Fire, Ice, Acid, and Heart

DANIELLE M. ORSINO

Fire, Ice, Acid, & Heart

A FAE Tale FROM THE VEIL

4 Horsemen
Publications, Inc.

Fire, Ice, Acid, and Heart
A Fae Tale from the Veil Book 1
Copyright © 2022 Danielle M. Orsino. All rights reserved.

4 Horsemen
Publications, Inc.

4 Horsemen Publications, Inc.
1497 Main St. Suite 169
Dunedin, FL 34698
4horsemenpublications.com
info@4horsemenpublications.com

Cover by Horsemen Publications, Inc.
Typesetting by Michelle Cline
Editor Jen Paquette

Map is illustrated by Daniel Hasenbos–he goes by Daniels Maps
"Kali" cover dragon illustration by PandiiVan
Dragon tournament illustration by Lavallion
Egg concept by Danielle M. Orsino
Egg illustration by PandiiVan

All rights to the work within are reserved to the author and publisher. No part of this publication may be reproduced, stored in a retrieval system, or transmitted in any form or by any means, electronic, mechanical, photocopying, recording, scanning, or otherwise, except as permitted under Section 107 or 108 of the 1976 International Copyright Act, without prior written permission except in brief quotations embodied in critical articles and reviews. Please contact either the Publisher or Author to gain permission.

This book is meant as a reference guide. All characters, organizations, and events portrayed in this novel are either products of the author's imagination or are used fictitiously. All brands, quotes, and cited work respectfully belong to the original rights holders and bear no affiliation to the authors or publisher.

Library of Congress Control Number: 2022936481

Print ISBN: 978-1-64450-593-9
eBook ISBN: 978-1-64450-592-2
Audio ISBN: 978-1-64450-589-2

Table of Contents

Chapter One:	Fire, Ice, and an Egg	1
Chapter Two:	The Tournament	22
Chapter Three:	Fire and More Fire	30
Chapter Four:	The Fight We Didn't Know We Were Waiting For	33
Chapter Five:	The Enemy of My Enemy	39
Chapter Six:	Acid vs. Fire or Love vs. Manipulation	45
Chapter Seven:	Game On	49
Chapter Eight:	Choices	64
Chapter Nine:	Opponent	71
Chapter Ten:	Heart	76
Chapter Eleven:	Rumble in the Ring	84
Chapter Twelve:	Blaze Battalion	99
Chapter Thirteen:	I'm In	103

DEDICATION

To all the animal lovers and
pet parents out there, this one is for you.

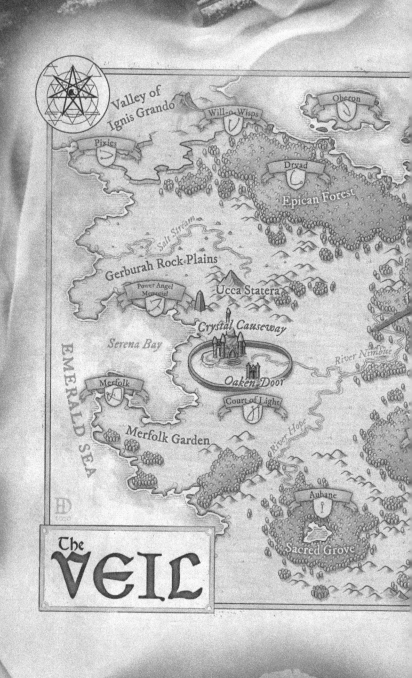

Acknowledgements

Jenn G & Kali: Thank you for allowing me the honor of using your love as inspiration for this story.

4Horsemen: Thank you.

The incomparable Pandiivan:
Thank you for your talent and artwork.

Carlos & Penelope: my own little furry muses.

Jenn & Whiskey
Jamie & Jasper
Denise & Pumpkin
Billy & Gemma
D.J. & Cherokee
Schaeffer, Digger, Maisie, & Skipper
Alan, Rene, & Momo
Christopher & Peaches
Ty & Bellatrix

Dr. Szabo: You wanted to be a dragon—here you go!

Author's Note

I want to take the opportunity to tell you the origins of this story as I believe it is important to know where you have come from to enjoy where you are going. Many of my Fae friends had been asking me for a dragon and Dark Fae–centric story, and I was happy to delve into the world of the Dark Fae and their dragons. However, the story really took shape when my best friend from high school, Jennifer—yes, the same one who inspired Lady Serena—told me of her beloved dog Kali's passing. As tribute to Kali, I named a dragon after her and put the two of them in a story. It was a quick story about a Dark Fae meeting a dragon who was allergic to snow pollen and their time training together.

I spoke with Jenn to receive her blessing and tried to capture Kali's personality; the story began to grow, and this novella was born. Jenn and Kali provided inspiration. I am grateful to both of them, just as I am grateful to my own pups, Carlos and Penelope, for the love and inspiration they give me every day.

This story is a love letter to all the pet parents out there whose day is a little better because of a wagging tail, a purr, a cold nose, or a serene aquarium. Whatever type of animal you give love to, enjoy it. Animals make the world a better place in so many ways. Jennara and Kali's story is all about having each other's back against all odds, experiencing unconditional love, and finding your home in those furry little faces.

Let the games begin!
~Danielle

This novella takes place after the events of *From the Ashes*, but before *Kingdom Come*.

Chapter One:
Fire, Ice, and an Egg

The horns announced first light, their baritone sound reverberating through Jennara's barracks. Morning formations were set to begin. The Dark Fae did not need the horn's blast letting her know it was time to get ready. Jennara had not slept. She had been up all night prepping the Kyanite armor Zucca had designed for her Fire-Breather, Kaliandra, Kali for short. Jennara had scrimped and saved for the purchase, but it was worth it. The armor covered the dragon's snout and nostrils, a new modification since their "little oops" when Kali had burned down an old armory shed. Some Fae can be so judgy! Besides other minor alterations to give them an edge, the rest of the armor was standard-issue, covering around her eyes and fire bladders, a vulnerable area in battle, as well as her chest and midback. Jennara had also paid extra to cover behind Kali's head; they weren't taking any chances.

This morning she and Kali would receive their invitation as rider and dragon to the Tournament of Fire, Ice, and Acid, an annual competition in which the Dark Fae selected one dragon-rider duo to join the elite ranks of the Blaze Battalion, the Ice Invaders, or the Acid Assault. Each High Council Guard nominated one team—rider and dragon—from their platoon to compete in the tournament. Jennara had been passed by for the last two years, but she had it on good authority that High Council Guard Yagora was nominating her and Kali to compete. *Today is our day.* She decided to take a walk and work off some of her nervous energy.

Jennara's walk took her to the Forest of Our Truth, a collection of quartz monuments that represented historical events for the Dark Fae. Truth about a civilization was not always pretty, and in the crystalline forest, all the good, bad, and in between of the Dark Fae was etched into the crystal pieces. Jennara paused at the smoky quartz pillars, reading the story of how King Jarvok had defeated Chief Peandro, leader of the Draconian Faction, in the battle of Fire, Ice, and Acid. Chief Peandro was sacrificing dragons he deemed sickly or useless to the Sacred Mountain in the name of their god. King Jarvok defeated Chief Peandro for control of the Draconians but had no interest in assuming the mantle. Dragor, Peandro's son, was set to inherit the tribes; however, in a tragic twist of fate, Dragor was one of the dragons due to be sacrificed that day. Dragor had not lit the Sacred Flame when his father asked him to, and thus had been deemed unworthy. Appalled, Jarvok gave Dragor the Draconian tribes as it was the dragon's birthright. Jarvok's one request was that the sacrificing of the dragons ceased.

One year later, Dragor had returned and lit the Sacred Flame, officially cementing his status as chief. The dragons had kept their freedom and the Dark Fae gained important friends and allies. When the Dark Fae went to war with the Court of Light, the dragons stood with the Court of Dark. Now, once a year, the Dark Fae came together in homage to the legendary battle between Jarvok and Peandro, holding a competition to choose the best among themselves to graduate to the elite fighting forces, all in the spirit of camaraderie and strengthening the bond between dragon and rider.

The monolithic crystals gleamed in the light now, the grey haze running through the center making the sigils stand out. Jennara ran her hands over the cool crystal.

Yes, today is our day.

She moved to a smaller crystal marker, where a dragon carved from clear quartz sat perched with his wings folded to his side. Jennara had been prepping for her trial for months. She had battled High Council Guard Pria in circle exercises and bested her. Lieutenant Zion had given her his approval, but he was not allowed to vote as he and Lieutenant Asa sat on the judges' panel. If it wasn't for Kali torching that armory shed during a sneezing fit, the pit in Jennara's stomach might not have her worried. *It wasn't Kali's fault.* Another Fae, Hausman—or Haus, as he was known—had dropped snow pollen in their ring, causing the reaction. Kali was highly allergic to snow pollen.

Haus was a competitive troll's prick, but it was more than that. He had told Jennara he liked destroying things, and he hoped King Jarvok and Queen Aurora's planned unification would not be a success. He wanted the war between the two courts to begin anew, and Haus would ride right next to the Dark Fae king as they rained fire, ice, and acid down on the Court of Light.

Jennara ran her fingers through her purple hair. She knew she had to push Haus' issues aside for now. Today was all about her and Kali—the two had worked so hard, and it was about to pay off. There were three special forces categories: the Blaze Battalion, the Acid Assault, and the Ice Invaders. The two would be competing for a spot in the Blaze Battalion, as Kali was a Fire-Breather. However, they would need to fight different types of dragons, not only Fire-Breathers, and this brought them to today. But before Jennara got ahead of herself, she needed to retrieve her invitation.

Jennara walked back into her barracks to get the Fire-Breather, knowing Kali was just as ready as she was. "Kali, wake up. Let's get our egg." Her love for the dragon ran deeper than any volcano.

The dragon stirred, yawned, and licked her lips. Her fire bladders pulsated. She stretched her front legs out, and her sickle tail snapped. The dragon stood, gave one final full-body stretch, and shook as the two headed out for lineup.

The High Council Guard members, Yagora, Pria, Azrael, Ezekiel, and Jonah, positioned themselves in the center of the main combat circle. DaVita was present for the ceremony too; her nickname was the Crystal Keeper since she constructed the dragon eggs. She was the Court of Dark's equivalent of the Court of Light's Malascola. Her artistry with crystals was legendary, but it was second only to her knowledge of crystals and how they helped with healing and weaponry. She was smaller in stature than some of the Dark Fae, but her arms were toned and cut from years of carrying large crystals and sculpting them into pieces of art. DaVita's icy-blond hair fell in soft waves to her back, gold and silver threads braided throughout, and the tips of her tresses were a kaleidoscope of pastel hues, from pale pink to sky blue. The open shoulders of her deep-green bell-sleeved top had amethyst crystals draped over the cutouts. DaVita's eyes flashed like labradorite; she was beautiful. She smiled with pride, knowing her artistic endeavors were about to make another Dark Fae's goals a reality. Her Ice-Breather, Jasper, stayed patiently by her side, glancing up at her intermittently as he guarded the five crystal boxes containing her work. The boxes were made of dragon jasper stone with iridescent swirls ranging from deep hunter green to light sage, complemented by a cherry-red background.

Lieutenant Zion stood over the boxes, hands behind his back; his dragon, Raycor, a large white Acid-Breather with black horns, sat to his right. Lieutenant Asa and her magenta Ice-Breather, Yanka, were to his left. King Jarvok and Dragor, the leader of the Draconian Faction, observed from the fortress window high above, Los the chameleon dragon watching along with them. Jarvok nodded at Zion.

Jennara pushed to the front of the crowd with Kali, ignoring the moans and groans. "Move, you goblin's ass," she mumbled as she made her way to the edge.

Lieutenant Zion gestured to his king.

The entire Dark Fae grouping swung their bodies toward the window, and each went to their right knee to acknowledge and give respect to their king. Raycor followed her rider with a call to the dragons, beating her wings; then Drake gave the first click, and a domino effect began as a hundred Fire-Breathers' back teeth sounded off and magenta fire blew upward into the air. The Ice-Breathers were next with waves of liquid ice shooting like geysers;

the Acid-Breathers continued to beat their wings because they could not safely spew their acid upward. Jarvok and Dragor bowed their heads simultaneously. Jarvok moved Los forward for the dragons to pay their respects to him, and they curved their necks. Finally, Dragor roared, calling the nomination process to order.

Zion gestured toward the first box. "High Council Guard Azrael nominates Hausman and his dragon, the Acid-Breather Famina, hailing from the western regions of Bahor Valley."

The tall Fae pushed past Jennara and smirked. He had long straw-colored hair braided with small bird skulls as decorations. His square jawline was battle scarred, but his whiskey-brown eyes locked on his trophy.

DaVita presented the box to Zion, who opened it; inside the box was a blue agate crystal egg. The object was shaped to resemble a dragon's egg and required two hands to hold it. The egg had three sides, each with its own petals, representing an oral defense for the dragons. The Fire side was inscribed with the sigil for Fire, and the petal was shaped like a growing flame. The Ice side bore the sigil for Ice; the petal had edges like icicles. Finally, the Acid side appeared bubbling, as if acid were dissolving the petal. This egg was the key to the tournament; the job of each team was to protect it. During the tournament, if a combatant or their dragon were hit, the egg would sustain the damage. For every three hits they took, one side of the egg opened. If all three sides opened, it was a forced hatch, and a tiny crystal dragon would emerge and fly away. Once that dragon appeared, the participant was disqualified. The other way to win was to steal an opponent's egg during the battle.

Jennara rolled her eyes. *Haus is a troll's prick, but a good fighter, and Famina is even better.* "Okay, no problem, Kali. Tough, but not impossible," she whispered to her dragon. Kali snorted.

Zion handed the egg to Hausman. "Do you accept this egg on behalf of High Council Guard Azrael?"

"Yes," Hausman replied with a bow of his head.

"Will you represent him, yourself, and your dragon in the Tournament of Fire, Ice, and Acid with the heart of the warrior, the fury of the storm and with honor above all else?"

Hausman glanced at his Acid-Breather, Famina, her light-blue wings outstretched as she chortled. He winked at her. "Yes, we will."

"I give you the first competitor for this rotation's Tournament of Fire, Ice, and Acid."

The crowd erupted into rhythmic stomping. Hausman and Famina moved to stand with Azrael, whose own Acid-Breather, Szabo, took his place by his rider's side.

Ezekiel's nominee was called out next. Mar and his Ice-Breather, Ogo, the eggplant-hued dragon with royal-blue tribal swirls, bounced up to stand next to his rider. Ogo was one of the younger dragons who had made a name for himself.

Jennara patted Kali's side. "Ogo is young and will be eager to prove his strength. We will have to be patient should we pull him in the first round." The dragon opened and closed her sickle tail in agreement.

Pria's choice followed: Grina and a second Acid-Breather, Tatcha. Tatcha was larger than Famina and a gorgeous shade of blush that reminded Jennara of the color the summer sky as the sun rises on the warmest of mornings. Her scales glittered, adding to the effect, and her deep-black horns had a hint of sheen. However, the dragon's beauty did not fool Jennara. Tatcha was ruthless. The Acid-Breather played up her looks to fool her opponents into thinking she was harmless; in fact, she enjoyed using her hollow canines to inject her acid into them while they were alive and listening to them scream as the acid dissolved their insides.

"All righty, Tatcha is a worthy opponent."

Kali gave a low rumble in response.

Jonah nominated a Fire-Breather, Ellis. The Fire-Breather was well skilled, although Jennara had beaten his rider, Sussex, in training exercises.

"Here we go..." Jennara rubbed her hands together and straightened her uniform. She turned and smoothed Kali's feathers. The dragon stood at attention. Jennara's platoon members gathered around, patting her on the back.

Lieutenant Zion picked up Yagora's box and lifted the lid, then glanced up. The group gasped. "High Council Guard Yagora, explain," Zion commanded.

Yagora stepped forward, face unreadable. Her hair was styled with the black left side cut short to above her ear and the white side long but plaited in small braids that joined in one long braid cascading down her back.

"Why is there no egg in your box?" Zion inquired.

"There was no Fae worthy this rotation, Lieutenant Zion."

Jennara's blood boiled. She stepped forward, but her platoon partner, Eywane, grabbed her and shook his head. Kali snapped her sickle tail in protest.

"How is that possible?" Asa asked, skepticism edging her voice.

Yagora stared ahead. "It is my platoon. I have full authority, do I not?"

"You do," Zion said.

"I will not nominate any of my soldiers to set them up for failure. I am being a pragmatic leader, as our king has taught us."

Zion glanced up toward his king, but Jarvok was no longer in view of the observation window. "Yagora, return to your place," Zion said. Through gritted teeth, he closed out the ceremony: "These are your nominees for the Tournament of Fire, Ice, and Acid. The games will begin tomorrow at the rising of the blood sun."

As the crowd cheered, Jennara's fellow platoon members patted her shoulder, unsure of what to say. Yagora did not make eye contact with her, but Jennara had something to say to the High Council Guard member.

As the crowd dispersed, Jennara and Kali headed straight for Yagora until Hausman blocked her path. "Oh, so sorry to hear I won't be kicking you and your dragon's ass tomorrow." He patted one of the bird skulls in his braid.

"Out of my way, Haus."

He glanced over his shoulder at Yagora, massaging his jaw. "You going to go cry to High Council Guard Yagora?" He changed his voice to a high falsetto and rubbed under his eyes with his knuckles, feigning a baby's cry. "Oh, why didn't you pick me? Wah, wah wah!"

Jennara's green eyes blazed. She dropped low, spinning, and swept his legs out from beneath him, sending the large Fae to the ground on his butt. She did not stop her momentum but continued her spin to stand and kept walking. Kali stepped over Haus but let her tail drag on him as she snorted, jerking her head at Famina.

"High Council Guard Yagora?" Jennara called, but Yagora and Pria had their heads together. They didn't even peek in her direction.

Haus shouted instead, "Get back here!"

Jennara rolled her eyes and exhaled. "Troll's balls," she mumbled.

Haus dusted himself off and stomped up to her. "That was a cheap shot—how dare you! That is why you weren't nominated. You are a crybaby and a dirty fighter. You are trying to throw the tournament by injuring me."

"Oh, please." Jennara sighed.

Kali growled and Famina snapped back, acid dripping from her canines, the ground beneath her beginning to smoke and dissolve from the acid pooling underneath.

Zion and Asa were walking away after the announcements but stopped when they heard the commotion. Asa whispered to Zion and the two paused for a moment and took a few steps back toward the gathering circle. They stayed about half a dragon's length away, just enough to observe and hear the exchange of name-calling. Azrael walked over to stand with them; still, Yagora and Pria did nothing.

Asa shot Zion a look.

"Let's see how this plays out," he replied.

A mixture of Haus' and Jennara's platoon members gathered.

"So what do you want, Haus? You want me to beat some manners into you right now? Because I'm not sure I have that much time. You are as thick-headed as a troll's back wart." She slapped her hands on her legs.

Haus' nostrils flared. "I am going to kick your ass right here, in front of your platoon and High Council Guard

Fire, Ice, and an Egg

Yagora so she can be vindicated for not nominating you. In fact, she will be so happy, she will throw her support to me."

Kali snapped her tail and roared at the insult, her plating compressing.

"Stop." The command came from above. A bellow echoed behind the command, and the dragons knelt. Dragor and Jarvok landed softly, kicking up a plume of dust.

The king dismounted his dragon. "Haus, you are confident in your skill?"

Haus dropped to his right knee. "Yes, my liege."

Jarvok paced, hands behind his back. "Azrael, are you confident in Haus?"

"I nominated him, my liege."

Jarvok raised his index finger to his lips. "Clever answer."

Haus' face scrunched up.

"Yagora," Jarvok called. "Do you have confidence in Haus to best Jennara?"

Yagora's head twitched. "I do not understand the nature of your question, my liege."

"It is simple: you did not nominate any soldier because you said it was not pragmatic. You would not want to set a soldier up for failure. Or is it they have not been trained properly? Do you feel confident Jennara will lose, and do you want to back Haus?"

Yagora glanced at Pria, knowing she was painted into a corner: if Yagora backed Haus, she was admitting she had not done her job, and if she backed Jennara, then why hadn't she nominated her?

"Well?"

"Ah, ah," Yagora fumbled.

"My liege?" Pria said. "I believe I have a way to settle this." The teal-haired Fae moved past her comrade. "It is clear Yagora does not want to embarrass Jennara and put her inadequacies on display. I have witnessed Yagora work with her; why, I myself allowed Jennara to best me in combat exercises to help with her confidence."

Jennara's eyes went wide with realization. Now she understood: she had humbled Pria in front of everyone, and the vain Fae had gotten her pride bruised, among other things. Yagora was paying her back for beating up her partner in crime. Worst of all, Pria was spinning it like she had let it happen. "I am a goblin's ass," Jennara mumbled under her breath.

"I think our little Jennara has gotten too big for her armor after our tussle if she believes she can take someone like Haus. Yagora asked me to take the fall and give her some confidence, and, well..." Pria pouted at Jennara. "It seems the plan worked too perfectly. If Yagora speaks up, she is afraid it would destroy what confidence the poor thing has."

Zion coughed to hide his laughter. "Since when does either of you two," he pointed at Yagora and Pria, "care about any Fae's feelings, or for that matter, if they have self-confidence?"

Dragor yawned, his jaw slamming shut.

Jarvok raised an eyebrow at the black dragon. "I concur with Dragor. I grow weary of this discussion, and I do not believe Pria's hypothesis. I will ask one more time: Yagora, do you back Haus?"

"Um... I wanted Jennara to have more faith in her fighting skill, so I asked Pria to fake—"

"*Enough!* Yes or no."

"Yes, my liege."

Jennara's eyes closed.

"Azrael, do you fully back Haus?"

"My liege, if Yagora is confident in Haus, I request the right to back Jennara." Azrael raised his chin as he gave his king the unorthodox answer.

Yagora's head snapped around. "What? Her dragon burned down the armory shed when you were on your courtship session with Aurora!"

Jarvok shrugged off Yagora's point. "Every Fire-Breather here has set something on fire, which is why all the important structures are stone, not wood. The armory shed was old."

"High Council Guard Azrael?" Haus pleaded.

"I feel Haus is capable, but I was present at the combat exercises in which Jennara bested Pria. I have seen Jennara in action, and I believe she and Kali are deserving of a chance. Given Haus has Yagora's support, she can give her egg to him, and mine can be given to Jennara and Kali. Will this be acceptable?"

Jarvok waved his hand. "I have no issues with this arrangement. Do you, Dragor?"

The Draconian chief stalked toward Kali, examining her from her navy and gold feathers to her fire plating down to her sickle tail. He sniffed the air around her. Kali followed her leader with her eyes, her tail twitching, and Jennara bit her bottom lip. Dragor clicked and clacked as Drake, a second Fire-Breather and a close confidant of Dragor, appeared. Drake trained most of the Blaze Battalion, so Dragor wanted the other dragon's opinion of this possible recruit.

Drake did not need or, more accurately, want a rider. If he did, he would only allow Jarvok or Asa to ride him. Drake was unusual; the rules of aging did not seem to apply to him. He was almost as old as Dragor, yet most of his body remained red, with only his tail all black. The Dark Fae were learning that what they knew of the Draconians was still evolving. In Drake's case, it was speculated he was a bastard son of Peandro and had chief blood, which was why Drake's coloring was different and his fire-breathing skills were so legendary. It was believed Dragor knew this as well and had brought him into the fold, keeping Drake as a close friend.

The two Fire-Breathers circled Kali, paying special attention to the area just behind her plating. They sniffed and exchanged small chirping sounds. Drake made a few sudden gestures with his neck, but Kali stood her ground.

Jennara dipped her head in an attempt to hide her smile. *That's my girl.*

Dragor gave Kali one final snort, and Drake clacked back at him. Then the Draconian leader clicked at Jarvok.

"Dragor accepts," the king said.

Jennara exhaled, winking at Kali.

Yagora stepped forward. "My liege, I—"

"It is settled. Haus, you will represent Yagora, and Jennara will represent Azrael. Zion, see the eggs are given to each of the nominees. I look forward to seeing both of you in the ring." Jarvok walked past Azrael, placing his hand on the High Council Guard's shoulder. "Nice to see you out of your forge and taking more of an interest in Fae things."

Azrael nodded, his eyebrows scrunched, confused…*"Haven't I been before?"*

Haus and Jennara bowed.

Jarvok and Dragor exited, Drake following behind.

"Yagora, retrieve your egg for Hausman," Asa commanded.

Yagora ran off, mumbling.

Haus sauntered up to Jennara, his voice a low growl. "I am going to wear your dragon as new boots when I am finished." He bit the air and walked away.

"Not while there is a drop of air in my lungs." Jennara grabbed Haus' wrist before he was out of reach. He attempted to shake her off, but she didn't release him. Worry flashed in his eyes. "My egg, Haus?"

He looked up. "Oh yes, of course. I was waiting for High Council Guard Yagora to return with *my egg*." He twisted his wrist free, using much more force than he needed. Jennara smiled sardonically.

Yagora appeared with the egg and presented it to Haus; Jennara took the one he had carried. The exchange was cold and efficient.

"Go and prepare for the tournament," Zion said, dismissing the Fae and their dragons.

Jennara showed the egg to Kali as if it could break or disappear at any moment. Two years of being passed over, and all the bruises and hours of training had culminated in this precious crystal object. She cradled it, running her fingers along the bands of blue and taupe, tracing the Fire sigil on the side before drawing the same symbol with her index finger along Kali's forehead. She cocked her head. "We need to see Zucca. I have one last alteration to make to your armor before tomorrow."

Jennara was about to head to the armory when Azrael caught her eye. She had almost forgotten about him, too lost in her thoughts. *Duh!* "Kali, this takes priority. Without him, we wouldn't be getting our chance." The dragon chortled. "Excuse me, High Council Guard Azrael, may I have a word with you?"

Azrael's lavender eyes with their black rings swung to meet hers. His chestnut-brown hair was pulled half up, the rest left long. The scar from his Angelite disc ran on a diagonal from right to left across his forehead. Azrael was as tall as Lieutenant Zion, but broader, as he had been the armory guard and blacksmith assistant for the Shining Kingdom when he was an Angel. Azrael was the only Power Brigade Angel to be gifted with the knowledge of how to imbue a Brigade member with an Elestial Blade. This skill had been taught to him by Archangel Michael, known as "the sword of the Creator." This was how Earthborn Dark Fae were able to have their own versions of Elestial Blades.

"Yes?" His voice was not as deep as one might expect it to be, given his size.

"Thank you." Jennara bowed, and Kali followed.

Azrael shook his head. "You do not owe me a thank you."

"But I do if it—"

He raised his palm. "I did not do this for you, Jennara."

Jennara paused, her brow crinkling. "I did not mean to insinuate preferential treatment."

"Nor did I. I did this for many reasons. In the High Council Guard, we are all equal. Yagora has no right to skirt the rules and traditions of the tournament, whatever her reasons are. I was present at your combat exercises. I told you I would back you if I could. The opportunity presented itself. I am a Fae of my word. You won the honor to compete, and I do not like it when any Fae is not given the chance they deserve. Let me be clear: I would not have taken it from Haus. As he is a competent and capable warrior, he warrants the chance to compete. However, I will not sit and watch this tournament be made a mockery of because Fae are letting personal feelings seep in. The

Fire, Ice, and an Egg

solution I suggested allowed for both you and Haus to compete."

"I understand." Jennara and Kali turned to leave.

"Oh, and Jennara?"

"Yes sir?" she answered over her shoulder.

"Be careful: you have three Fae whose egos you have bruised. That doesn't put the odds in your favor. A male Fae whose ego you damaged is one thing, but female Fae who have egg on their face, excuse the pun..." He waved his hand dismissively as if embarrassed by the awkward play on words. "They are dangerous, more than an Acid-Breather with a toothache."

Jennara stiffened her spine and lifted her chin, turning to face him.

Azrael held up an index finger as he spoke. "Some of us bond with Ice-Breathers for their cold, calculating temperament or Acid-Breathers for their ruthlessness. I bonded with Szabo, an Acid-Breather; he has a shrewd demeanor, but make no mistake, he is ferocious. I have heard many avoid Fire-Breathers because they can be more temperamental, or they have an ego. Look at Drake—he is one of the only dragons who still refuses to fully bond with a rider, and he is a Fire-Breather—"

Jennara scratched behind Kali's fire plating, her green eyes meeting Azrael's lavender gaze. "Well, I didn't seem to have an issue, nor do I scare easily." Kali snapped her sickle tail shut to emphasize her rider's point, and they walked away.

The side of Azrael's mouth turned up. "Chaos be with both of you," he whispered.

As Kali's tail sank over the hill, Azrael felt the power push crawl over whatever flesh was not covered by Kyanite armor. He had counted on Yagora having something to say. "Voice your displeasure, Yagora."

"What makes Jennara so special that she got the almighty former right hand of Archangel Michael out of his forge? Does she know her way around the hilt of a sword, perhaps?"

Azrael rolled his eyes. "Oh, please, Yagora. I am not even going to entertain such an immature accusation. I nominate a Fae every cycle."

"And none have ever made it past the first round. You may have had a shot with Haus, but with Jennara, no. Will you aura-blend with her tonight when she is grateful or go to her after she loses and provide her some comfort? When was the last time you aura-blended with any Fae?" Yagora shook her head.

"I will do no such thing, and if you continue to insinuate so, I will tell Lieutenant Zion exactly why you did not nominate Jennara and Kali." Azrael pointed at her.

Yagora's sarcastic demeanor melted away, her black eyes flashing red. "I already said I do not feel she is ready," she growled.

"No. Jennara humiliated your lover, Pria, and you are punishing her for it."

"That is—"

Azrael pivoted like a viper on Yagora. "I was present, and whether Pria underestimated Jennara or not is irrelevant. You concocted a story to save face. Pria *was* an amazing fighter, but she has you to protect her, and she has become soft. You do everything for her—she snaps her fingers, and you go running. Pria got her ass handed to her by Jennara, and you should have been thrilled. Yagora, you trained Jennara! That sweep is one of your signature moves.

By all that is light in the universe, Yagora, look at yourself—you gave up one of your own for Pria! What does she do for you?" Yagora pursed her lips as Azrael stepped closer. "How many times have you killed or slain and Pria has taken the credit? I have seen you run her platoon through formations while she sleeps. Why?"

"Because I love her with all my heart!" Yagora yelled and glanced around as her outburst caught unwanted attention. "She knows I'm a terrible Fae. She doesn't care. She accepts me." The last sentence was barely a whisper.

Azrael exhaled, and with his breath, some of his anger toward Yagora evaporated too. "Oh, my friend, you aren't a terrible Fae. You are in love with the wrong Fae. That's all."

Yagora's gaze flew up to meet his; she unsheathed her Elestial Blade and pointed it under his chin. The light highlighted the surprise in his eyes as his eyebrows reached for his hairline. "How dare you. You don't know Pria like I do! I am terrible, Azrael, and you would be wise to remember that. I don't know why you care now. Go back to your forge. You never get involved in these sorts of issues. Do not start now. We were fine without you."

Azrael stared at Yagora's Auric weapon blazing, charged with her emotions. He bit the inside of his cheek. *Would she use it on me? Is it all for show? I hit a nerve. Best not to test her.*

He rubbed his temples. "Fine, sure, Yagora, you are a horrible Fae. Is that what you want to hear? Pria is the best thing for you. I hope you two are happy. Just remember this moment, how her *love* caused you to pull out your blade on someone who has known you for your entire life. Yeah, that sounds like true love."

Yagora's breath came fast, but she flicked her wrist and the light disappeared. "I said terrible, not horrible—*terrible*. You are a troll's prick, Azrael. No one has heard from you in years. You toil away in your forge, only coming out when Jarvok calls you for meetings. No one sees you, so do not speak of friendship. You know nothing of love. You have spent far too much time around weapons and are incapable of emotion. Steel will never break your heart, which is why you surround yourself with it. Archangel Michael taught you well."

He nodded at the accuracy of her strike. "You always knew how to recognize where someone is most vulnerable. Enjoy the tournament." Azrael walked away.

Yagora glanced over her shoulder at Pria, who was deep in conversation with Grina while Tatcha stood watch. Pria was twirling her teal hair around her finger and glancing up through her lashes at Grina.

Damn, I know that look. Is it the dragon or Grina? The only thing Pria loves more than aura-blending is power. Yagora watched Pria stroke the pink dragon's neck. *Yup, it's the power.* Yagora exhaled, defeated.

Jennara walked in quiet contemplation through the crowd as Fae congratulated her. Azrael's words danced around her mind. Kali nudged her. "I know, girl. I am not so worried about Haus. He is a goblin's ass, but he will be emotional, and it can work to our advantage. Tatcha is a whole different story. Grina, she is formidable, but her long-range weapon skills aren't up to par. She is a good grappler, decent even, and let's face it, I am better with my stand-up game." The Fire-Breather nodded and gave a snort. "We can't have it go to a no-hit against them. I think we will need to keep the boundary line intact with Grina. Tatcha cannot spit her royal acid for long periods or distances before she has to resort to her regular acid, so the boundary lines will work for us. Hit first and fast will have to be our strategy if we pull them in the first round."

Kali chortled.

"What? You have a better plan?"

The dragon clicked and clacked her teeth.

"Well, I would like to see the pink dragon get eliminated too, but I don't think that is going to happen. You heard Azrael—we pissed off a lot of Fae. I have a funny feeling Pria is going to arrange that Tatcha and Grina get the bye. You and I, my friend, are going to be fighting all three rounds—if we win at all." Jennara rubbed her eyes and held her head. "Oh, Kali, what did I do? I was all hyped like a troll on snow pollen, and now..." She shook her head and looked into Kali's deep brown-and-gold eyes. The dragon licked her face, her black tongue leaving Jennara damp.

Jennara wiped the dragon's saliva from her eyes and winked one eye open. Kali was grinning, and Jennara could not be upset with the Fire-Breather after a vote of confidence like that. Blinking back the wetness, Jennara giggled. "Okay, I got it. We are in this together. But next time give me a warning. Especially after you have eaten cod. Yuck." She shivered.

The dragon rolled her eyes and belched.

"Seriously, Kali?"

Chapter Two:
The Tournament

The nominees lined up shoulder to shoulder, their dragons behind them. They raised their chins in unison toward the growing light, creating sharp noble profiles. The Ice-Breathers' vapor exhales sent ribbons of condensation through the morning air like fog. The red sun rising over the peak of Blood Haven touched the golden tunnel of light illuminating the light-blue sky—the perfect representation of a flame. The blood sun happened once a year, a natural elemental spectacle when the Sacred Mountain and the surrounding acid geysers erupted together for a brief period overnight. The acid and ash particles the geysers threw up into the air were so forceful, they turned the sun red the following morning. The Draconians had once used that day to sacrifice their sickly ones, and now it had become the day of the tournament. A day of new beginnings, the morning of the blood sun.

The nominees waited in the center of the coliseum located at the far end of the fortress' bounds. Dark Fae filed in toward the benches. An empty platform waited at

The Tournament

the other end of the arena, where banners of each faction waved silently above the platform. Around the platform were wooden perches for the dragons.

A loud horn sounded, and Raycor landed on the first perch with a roar; ten Acid-Breathers in White Kyanite armor dropped from the sky, the original members of Acid Assault. The dragons and their riders lined up to the left as Lieutenant Zion took his place on the platform. He nodded, and the arena erupted into chants.

Yanka took her place on the perch as the horn sounded twice. Five Ice-Breathers wearing Blue Kyanite armor landed in a domino fashion, the first Ice Invaders. Lieutenant Asa walked across the platform to stand next to Zion, accompanied by the roars of the dragons.

Finally, the horn sounded three times, and Drake sat on a perch to the left of the platform. He clacked his back teeth as ten Fire-Breathers circled the coliseum and in unison drew the sigil for the Draconian Faction with fire in the sky. The purplish-magenta flames lit the morning sky ablaze. As they finished their breath of fire, the dragons zigzagged past each other to land. These were the first of the Blaze Battalion, armed in their Green Kyanite armor.

Finally, King Jarvok entered as Dragor arrived from above, settling on the tallest post. The High Council Guard stood to the right, straight and tall, their dragons on their perches.

The chief of the Draconians roared, and all the dragons answered.

King Jarvok held his hands up to the crowd. "My kin, today we meet to honor those who have shown extreme dedication to improving their skills. Now they will test these skills in our time-honored tradition of combat.

Today, we will see which dragon and rider are worthy of the honor of being named one of the elite. Chaos be with you. Let the tournament begin!"

The entire arena erupted into chants of "Chaos be with you!"

Zion stepped forward to review the rules of the tournament. "Each dragon and rider must work together to protect their egg and each other to win their match."

Los held up a blue agate crystal egg next to Zion to demonstrate.

"There are two ways to win the match," Zion said. "First, a forced hatching. Each Fae's armor and their dragon's armor are attuned to each other's aura, the boundary lines, and the egg. If either takes a hit or steps over the boundary lines before it is allowed, the egg will register it. Three hits, and one side of the egg opens. Nine hits, and the egg will hatch—a baby dragon will emerge from the egg and fly to the judges, signaling the egg no longer needs protecting and the match is over. The nominee has lost. Another possibility is forced hatching by knockout when either the rider or dragon sustains a hit strong enough to render them unconscious."

Los opened the egg and took the baby crystal dragon out, mimicking the flying motion of the creature. Zion glanced down at Los, who offered the crystal dragon up to him. Zion shook his head. Giggling came from the crowd.

Zion cleared his throat. "The second way to win is to steal the egg. After one minute, if neither nominee has been hit, the boundary line is erased, and you can cross the line to steal your competitor's egg, but the stand will disappear and reappear every thirty seconds. The nominees have no control over their eggs."

The Tournament

Los continued pantomiming the rules, much to the enjoyment of the crowd. His tongue lolled to the side.

Zion slid Los a look of disapproval, but Zion knew when he was beat. Los was a crowd favorite. "The eggs remain locked on the stand until the final round, in which the nominee will face a dragon and rider of Dragor's choosing, and the rules will change depending upon whether there is a hit in the first minute. If not, the eggs will be carried by the competitors and can be taken by force and must be delivered to the platform."

Dragor flapped his wings in acknowledgment. Los flew around, ramping up the crowd.

Haus dragged a finger across his throat, looking at Jennara. She shook her head and rolled her eyes. Kali snapped her tail at Famina, who thrashed back. The other nominees sensed the building anxiety and reacted too, twitching and shuffling.

Zion's sapphire eyes flicked side to side. "Nominees, we now take the oath. Riders, present your eggs."

The nominees stepped forward with their eggs over their heads. Then they went down on one knee as their dragons bowed their heads. The crowd was silent.

"Riders and dragons, you have been chosen to represent your platoon, faction, and commanders. Do you swear to compete with integrity, perseverance, honor, and indomitable spirit?"

The nominees and dragons all replied in harmony, "I do."

"Chaos be with you." Zion gestured to King Jarvok.

The king stood and walked to the edge of the platform. "Let the tournament begin!"

Fire, Ice, Acid, and Heart

The sound from the crowd was deafening. The nominees moved to the side as their respective platoons waved banners with the riders' and dragons' names on it.

Haus took the opportunity to bump into Jennara. "I am going to enjoy kicking your ass," he said.

Jennara did not reply; instead she whispered to herself, "I am one with my dragon; my dragon is one with me. Together, we are one mind, one set of wings, and one sword."

Asa looked over the nominees lined up on the side. Then she nodded to Los, who flew up and removed a sheet covering a wooden slatted sign with the bracket divisions.

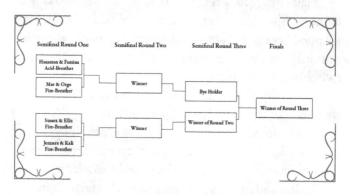

The crowd gasped at the revelation. As predicted, Grina and Tatcha had gotten the bye, so the two would not see action until the third round.

Kali swished her tail.

"It's okay, girl. We got this," Jennara whispered. The dragon glanced up, and Jennara winked.

"Round one competitors, take your places," Asa said.

Yagora sat on Hausman's side of the ring, and Ezekiel on Mar's side. Each commander would lend strategic words of encouragement during the match. The other competitors sat on a long wooden bench, awaiting their turn.

Zion commanded the competitors to place their eggs on the safeguards. Haus and Mar went to the back of their rings and, with the assistance of their dragons, carefully put the eggs on the floating gold staffs. The staffs were ten feet tall, carved with the sigil for the Draconian Faction and the elemental symbols for Fire, Ice, and Acid, and inlaid with crystals. The top fanned out to house the crystal eggs, with a stunning crystal moonstone crescent moon rising in the back to support the egg. There was an audible click as the eggs settled in.

Haus lined up closest to the boundary line with Famina staying back to protect the egg. Mar and Ogo did the opposite. Ogo's ice tusk scales flipped erratically as vapor wisps escaped. His tail swished side to side.

"Easy, big guy," Mar reminded his dragon.

Haus' eyes narrowed. Famina was perfectly still.

"Fight!" Zion yelled. The horn sounded, and the crowd came alive.

Plasma balls flew across the boundary lines from the two Dark Fae. The dragons rolled and dodged. Ogo breathed his icy defense as Haus backflipped out of the way, and the ice made a patch of icicles, which Haus broke off and used as a spear to throw at Mar. Famina flapped her wings to break the rest off and send them reeling toward Ogo. Haus followed up immediately with a plasma ball. Mar and Ogo were still trying to recover from Famina's wing storm when the spear hit Ogo in the chest, the plasma ball hitting Mar next.

"Double hit!" Zion called.

The Acid side of the egg glowed. Haus smirked and Famina chortled. The crowd cheered and stomped. Haus and Famina ramped up their assault—she used her wings, and Haus jumped and twisted, throwing more plasma balls, using her wing wind to propel the balls at the other two.

Mar and Ogo were on the defense now, trying to get a plasma ball off themselves, but Haus and Famina were relentless. Ogo switched positions with Mar and backed up to the egg, blowing a sheet of ice to hide behind, but Famina went up to the boundary and spit her regular acid to dissolve the ice while Haus kept Mar busy.

Then Zion yelled, "Acid side is open!" The egg glowed, each band of color illuminated, and the Acid petal cracked and unlocked.

"Ahhh!" Mar screamed in frustration, realizing he was the one hit.

Haus growled; he had them against the ropes and he knew it. "Now, Fam!"

The dragon opened her massive wings, lowering her neck as Haus backflipped to land on her head. He pulled his hands apart, and the smell of ozone grew pungent, the plasma ball growing bigger and bigger. Energy sparked and popped. Mars and Ogo stared in awe. Famina rose to her full height as the energy ball became the size of Haus' chest. Ogo tried to create a shield of ice, but it was futile; Haus raised the plasma orb and Famina spit her acid to break the ice shield, and the gigantic plasma orb hit both Mar and Ogo, knocking them unconscious. Mar's armor sustained a good portion of the damage, but the left side of his face bubbled, burned by the plasma.

The egg lit up; the top opened, and a small crystal dragon shot out and flew to Jarvok's waiting palm. He closed his hand and stood. "Forced hatching due to knockout! Haus and Famina—winner!"

Once the shock wore off, the crowd was jubilant, chanting Haus' and Famina's names. Yagora glanced at Azrael with a smug look.

The healers ran out to gather Mar and Ogo out of the ring and ready it for round two.

Chapter Three:
Fire and More Fire

Jennara and Kali walked into the ring. "Well, girl, this is it." Kali snapped her tail, and Jennara paused as if she suddenly realized the scope of the coliseum. "Kali, look at this place." Jennara felt her mouth fall open. Kali chortled. "I know, my head is in the game, but wow, I didn't notice it before. I mean, we are here." She turned to the dragon and hugged her. The two danced in a circle, jumping up and down.

Azrael looked from the sidelines in utter disbelief. "What is she on? Jennara!" he called out. But the two of them were so busy doing their little celebration dance, they did not hear him. Azrael glanced up at Jarvok, who was looking around at the others with either amusement or disdain—Azrael couldn't tell, and that wasn't a good sign.

Kali was now shaking her sickle tail, and Jennara was hip-bumping her to a song obviously only the two of them could hear in their heads. Jennara sang, "We made it, dun, dun, dun, da, da."

Fire and More Fire

Dragor roared, and Jarvok spoke. "Are you two done? Or should I get the band in here to accompany you?"

Jennara and Kali froze mid-dance. "So sorry, my liege. We are just very excited."

Jarvok fought a smile. "I can see that, but we do have a tournament to get on with, so as entertaining as this is," he rolled his wrist, "would you mind if we continued?"

Azrael slapped his forehead as he watched Jennara's scolding. Yagora laughed at him.

"Of course, my liege." Jennara bowed, and Kali followed suit.

"I hope you fight better than you sing and dance, Jennara," Zion said.

Jennara winced and took her place with Kali, ready to fight.

This fight started much slower than the match before; the two Fire-Breathers were more cautious, their sickle tails snapping back and forth at each other. Whichever one breathed fire first would be left vulnerable because it took the dragon a minute to recover and allow their fire bladders time to refill. This meant it was up to the riders to make the first move.

"Competitors, you have thirty seconds or the boundary line will be erased," Asa announced.

Jennara smirked and glanced at Kali. Understanding flowed between them—this was what the two wanted.

Sussex rushed forward and threw a plasma ball the two easily dodged.

"Lazy technique. We got him acting emotionally," Jennara mumbled. "Perfect!"

Asa called out, "Erase the line! The staffs will now move at random."

"Kali, guard the egg!"

The Fire-Breather nodded and backed up as the staff disappeared and reappeared ten feet away to the left.

Sussex took the part of egg guardian and sent his dragon, Ellis, to square off against Jennara. But she flipped out of the way when his magenta fire streamed toward her. As the dragon reloaded, she gathered her energy, making eye contact with Kali. They had practiced this trick, and now was the time to try it. Jennara rushed Ellis, building her plasma orb. As Ellis breathed fire at Jennara, she caught it in the forming plasma and closed the orb with the fire inside, then threw it up in the air. Kali swatted it with her tail, sending it hurtling back like a meteor at Sussex—a direct hit. Sussex flew across the ring. Ellis rushed to check on his rider. Kali scooped up Jennara and the two made a play for the egg, grabbing it.

"Egg captured! Flawless performance. Winner—Jennara and Kali."

Jennara raised her arms in victory and Kali spewed fire straight up into the air. The Dark Fae's gaze slid toward Haus, who was seething on the side, pacing, his nostrils flaring and his fists balled.

Jennara smirked, figuring Haus would be next with the way her luck had been going. However, that was the thing about luck; you never knew whose side it truly was on.

Chapter Four:
The Fight We Didn't Know We Were Waiting For

"Next round, Haus and Famina versus," Zion paused and the arena was silent, "Grina and Tatcha!"

The Fae went crazy with the news of two Acid-Breathers fighting. Banners flew; the coliseum sounded like an ocean during a storm.

Haus glanced at Jennara and snarled as he ran into the ring.

Jennara had assumed Grina and Tatcha wouldn't fight until the last semifinal round, but she was incorrect. Grina had only received the bye for the first round.

"Haus and Famina, place your egg. Grina and Tatcha, do the same," Zion commanded.

"Looks like we have a reprieve," Jennara said as she cleaned the dust from Kali's armor. She wasn't sure if she was relieved or not. Something in her gut was twisting, and she couldn't shake it. "Kali, why do I have a bad feeling?"

The dragon snapped her tail, indicating she knew something was off too.

"Maybe it's just the adrenaline from the last fight. I mean, it is Haus and Grina, Pria's and Yagora's nominees. Probably the safest match out of all of us. I am being dramatic."

Out on the field, the two Acid-Breathers sat stretching their wings in a demonstration of dominance.

Jennara shook her head. "Kali, this is going to be messy. I take it back—this is not the safest match."

The Fire-Breather snorted, watching the other dragons.

Tatcha had calmed suddenly, tucking her wings to her body, unmoving now. Gone was the alpha display from a few moments ago; perhaps she had done it to see if Famina would follow suit or to rile the other dragon up, expend her energy. Tatcha stood steadfast now, her blush-colored scales glittering in the sunlight like starfish in shallow tide pools. However, her serenity was the calm in the sea before a tsunami—when all the water drained from the shoreline as the wave was forming.

Famina paced back and forth, her light-blue scales rippling as she moved. Her black horns did not look as regal as Tatcha's as they snaked with her head in a show of agitation. No, Tatcha had an air of confidence the other dragon could not match, no matter how many intimidating moves Famina made.

Grina twirled finger knives, her feet apart, knees soft and eyes focused. She stood only a few feet in front of her dragon; she was centered and ready.

Haus appeared keyed up like his dragon. His leg was shaking, his eye twitching, and his lips twisting into a sneer.

The Fight We Didn't Know We Were Waiting For

"This match will determine who advances to the third round of the semifinals," Zion announced with more of a command to his voice to establish the depth and breadth of the situation. The competitors didn't look at the second-in-command; their eyes were locked on each other.

This had the makings of a bloodbath. The only saving grace was that both dragons were Acid-Breathers, so their acid bite would not have the same effects as it did on other dragons. It would hurt like hell, but the acid would not dissolve them from the inside out.

The horns sounded, and the fight was on. Plasma orbs flew about, the smell of ozone filling the air. Both dragons took to the sky, staying on their respective sides. Famina spewed acid while Tatcha was graceful in her avoidance.

Grina and Haus were throwing everything they could at each other.

"No hits. Competitors, the boundary line is erased," Asa announced.

Haus and Famina charged forward, crossing the now-defunct boundary line in an attempt to put Grina and Tatcha on the defense.

The blush dragon and hot-pink-mohawk-haired Dark Fae backed up in a staggered formation, Grina taking the lead. Haus picked up his speed as he pulled a small clear quartz ball from his pocket. It was smooth but warm. He smiled at Famina. He recalled Yagora telling him, "It is not illegal, just frowned upon" during their strategy meeting the previous day.

Haus had thought he would be using it on Jennara, but he was confident he didn't need any tricks for her. Besides, he wanted to end this fight with Grina and Tatcha now. He chucked it at the pair, and as the ball rolled toward them, Haus glanced at Famina, yelling, "*PrakAza*," their signal for light. Famina turned her face as the quartz ball exploded into a bright blinding light.

But at the same time, Tatcha and Grina hit a button on the side of their armor, and visors came down over their eyes. The two were completely unaffected by the flash-bang.

"How the hell did she know?" Haus mumbled. He scanned the sidelines and locked eyes with Yagora, who turned her head quickly. Her look of guilt was evident. "You?" he mouthed. Nearby, Pria stood arrogant and confident. Everything crystallized for Haus. Yagora had told her lover about their plan; she had figured he would use the trick on Pria's choice rather than saving it for Jennara. She had warned Pria, and Grina was prepared. That was why he was fighting them now. Yagora would feed Pria info, and Jennara would be an easy victory too. "Troll's balls," he muttered.

Then Tatcha charged him, her head down, horns gleaming in the light, picking up steam with every step. Famina stepped in the way to protect her rider. The two Acid-Breathers tussled while Haus rolled out of the way, forgetting about his egg, the plumes of dirt clearing as the dragons clashed. Their horns locked as they pushed each other back and forth like rams. Growls emanated from deep inside each dragon each time one would gain the dominant position. Finally, Tatcha twisted right and broke free, then roared and bit down on Famina's neck.

Haus screamed and ran forward as his dragon let out her own scream of pain. Famina's fistula extended, and her royal acid discharged in reflex, hitting Haus in the face. His Kyanite battle armor was only able to shield him for so long before the smoke rose, and her acid ate through it. He dropped to the ground, covering his eye and rolling around.

Grina grabbed the egg.

Haus yanked the dissolving helmet off his face, bits of skin sticking to the suede inside. His helmet had no face shield, just smaller eye openings and a nose bridge protector, and the acid splash had landed in his eye. A scream of agony ripped from deep within his essence, true sadness, not pain. He threw the helmet down, revealing his eye was gone, eaten away by his own Acid-Breather's oral defense.

The sound may have been the reason Tatcha released Famina. She left the other dragon unconscious on the ground and stalked above in a victory walk.

"Egg captured!" Zion announced, but his voice did not have its earlier tenor.

The crowd was not thrilled with the win either. The sight of Haus' injury and Famina's limp body was too much.

Asa yelled for a healer, but she was already attending to Haus. Holding his head in her lap, she looked at the empty eye socket.

"How is Famina?" he asked in a strained voice.

Asa glanced over her shoulder at the two dragons helping Famina. "She is being taken care of."

Haus squeezed Asa's hand. "Please don't let Fammy see me hurt. I don't want her to know it was her acid. She didn't mean to."

Asa nodded. "Where is the lightforsaken healer?" she screamed as Haus' eye socket collapsed like a sinkhole in the ground.

The healer arrived with a gurney, and Haus was moved out of the ring, Famina behind him carried by the dragons.

"We will reset the ring before the third round of Grina and Tatcha versus Jennara and Kali," Zion announced.

Jennara watched as Haus was carried past. His good eye held hers, but his expression lacked malice.

Jennara tilted her head; his gaze did not waver. "Kali, am I crazy, or do you think Haus wants to talk to me?"

The Fire-Breather glanced from her rider to the figure being loaded into the tent. Her sickle tail snapped shut.

"Yeah, I think so too." Jennara bit her bottom lip. She started to walk away but pivoted back toward the healer's tent. She couldn't let this go. "Come on. We have a few minutes."

Chapter Five:
THE ENEMY OF MY ENEMY

Inside the tent, a healer in a long, soft-green tunic with gold tassels on the shoulders prepped a tonic. Metallic rose-gold threads looped like waves from the ocean down the front of the tunic. His boots were silent as he walked over and laid a compress on Haus' eye. Jars of herbs and salve sat open on a table next to the cot. An apprentice in an unadorned lavender robe puttered around, cleaning up after the healer. Jennara pressed herself against the tent wall, trying to stay out of the way as she watched the healer work on Haus.

She swallowed. This Fae was her enemy a little while ago, and she had questioned whether he was close to becoming a Weeper. Now he looked broken. He was covered in dirt and dust from the ring, and half his Kyanite armor had been removed and piled up in the corner. The right side of his body had smaller compresses covering the burns from where the acid had eaten through his pants. Haus' face was most startling, though. The bandage hid much of the damage, but he was pale. *No, not pale, almost grey.*

The healer checked the compresses one last time, then nodded at Jennara and exited the tent, followed by the apprentice.

"Um, Haus?" Jennara brought her hand to her lips as her voice cracked.

Haus blinked his left eye open. "Jennara? Good you came." He raised his left hand, beckoning her closer, and reached for her.

Jennara stepped forward to take his clammy hand. "I am here. Why did you want to see me, Haus?" She grimaced at her choice of words.

Haus coughed and laughed. "Still a pain in my ass. But I wanted to warn you. Yagora told Pria my strategy. She knew about my flash-bang. They aren't counting on you being a threat, so be careful, Jennara. I wanted it to be you and me at the end, but Yagora will do anything for Pria, including throwing the tournament. That's not what we stand for. Fammy is my kin, and now..." He choked up, releasing her hand to cover his mouth. Jennara looked away for a moment. "Don't underestimate Grina, Yagora, or Pria," he said. "Just go out and fight like Lucifer is on your tail! Chaos be with you." He turned his head.

Jennara straightened her shoulders. "I will, Haus." She touched his leg.

"Kick that bitch's ass like I know you can," he mumbled.

As Jennara opened the flap of the tent, Azrael stood blocking her way.

"High Council Guard Azrael, I was checking on Haus."

Azrael arched an eyebrow. "You were concerned about Haus? You two like each other about as much as a troll likes a Gnome. Nice try."

Jennara slumped her shoulders. "Haus needed to talk to me."

Azrael made a rolling gesture with his wrist, his gauntlets creaking with the motion. "And..."

"If I tell you, I will be breaking his trust."

Azrael grabbed her arm and threw her up against an armory shed. "Do you think this is a game, Fae? Famina is in critical condition—her main royal acid vesicle has been punctured! Haus lost his eye. In all the time of this tournament, we have never had a casualty or injuries of this magnitude. There was always a rule of no kills. Dragor and Raycor are ready to fight over this. Tatcha is feigning innocence for her savagery toward Famina. We both know flash-bangs are not illegal, but why on earth Haus decided to use one is beyond me, so if you have information, talk! Or else you and Kali might not be so lucky."

Jennara shook her arm loose and removed her helmet. "Okay, okay. Haus said he thinks Commander Yagora told Pria about his strategy, I guess technically *their* strategy. Yagora knew about his flash-bang, and they weren't counting on me being a threat. He thinks Yagora will do anything for Pria, including throwing the tournament."

Azrael backed up, his hand cupping his chin. "Are you sure that is exactly what he said?" There was a piercing light behind Azrael's eyes.

"Yes, of course. Haus didn't elaborate, but those were his words. Now I have to get back to the ring."

The High Council Guard shook his head. "There is no need to rush. Didn't you hear me? Dragor and Raycor are ready to fight. Jarvok has his hands full with them. Other dragons are trying to dampen the acid Famina spit everywhere. You aren't fighting just yet."

"Why are Dragor and Raycor at odds?" Jennara asked.

Azrael shook the dust from his cape. "Famina is badly injured, and if she loses her acid vesicle, she can't spawn. She was due to mate this season. Dragor did not want any eligible mating females competing in the tournament for fear of injury. Raycor never agreed with the rule and pushed for Famina's entry. Ever since the Massacre of Secor Valley, Dragor has had a different point of view on female dragon kin."

Jennara nodded in understanding. "So, we go and explain what happened."

Azrael puffed out his cheeks as he exhaled. "With what proof? Haus' statement? Please, Jennara, think!" He pointed to his temple. "Yagora and Pria thought this out. Yagora put the flash-bang in Haus' hand, knowing it was frowned upon, but baited him to use it against you. She knew he wouldn't wait to use it. He is far too impetuous. His goal was to fight you, and he would do anything to get to the final round with you—they played him like a fiddle. If Haus says Yagora told him to use it, that is his word against a High Council Guard's. He will look like a sore loser."

Jennara shrugged. "That doesn't explain why Grina and Tatcha had visors in their tournament armor. Surely that proves the flash-bang theory."

"No. It shows Pria was suspicious of Haus' machinations and prepped her nominee well—that's all."

"By all that is light in the universe." Jennara kicked the dirt. "Now what do I do?"

Azrael grabbed her head and steadied her, staring into her eyes. "Look at me!" His gaze was fire and ice. Jennara glanced up and put her hands over his. "I know you can do this," he said. "You are going to show them who they are messing with. That they can't step over you. You, Jennara, have earned this spot with Kali. Now go and win. Chaos be with you." He released her and angled his chin, gesturing for her to leave.

Jennara squared her shoulders, blading her body, hands in fists by her side, and looked toward the ring. Her purple hair blew in the wind, and when she turned back, a sneer grew along her lips. "Chaos be with you, Azrael." She called for Kali. The Fire-Breather, never far away, emerged from beside the medical tent. "Come, my friend. We have a match to win."

Something on Kali's armor caught Azrael's eye, two sigils inscribed on the dragon's helmet above the bridge of her snout, but it was too quick for him to make it out. He raised his hand to call them back and ask but decided against it. Azrael lifted his face skyward and repeated the Dark Fae blessing: "Chaos be with you, Jennara and Kali."

Chapter Six:
Acid vs. Fire or Love vs. Manipulation

Jennara and Kali arrived at the ring, propelled with vengeance for Haus and Famina. "I can't believe I am thinking about Haus and how he was wronged," Jennara whispered to Kali, and the Fire-Breather's tail waved as her eyes rose to the Dark Fae; she let out a long chortle in agreement and disbelief. "I agree, girl," Jennara said. "Yagora is wrong regardless of Haus being a troll's prick, and Famina didn't deserve—"

A roar erupted from Dragor, and the two turned their heads in time to see a huge dust cloud. Kali opened her wings to help block the debris, shielding her rider.

Through the wall of dust, two large dragon figures could faintly be made out. Raycor's pearlescent body was easier to see than Dragor's smoky black outline, but the snapping sound of the Draconian chief's large sickle tail reverberated throughout the arena. Grains of sand and ground-up crystal fell and caught the light, almost ethereal, like tiny falling stars. However, the meeting between them was anything but peaceful. Dragor's fire plating began to compress with his breathing; Raycor's forked tongue lifted as she readied her acid fistula.

"Oh Kali, this is so not good! If they fight over Yagora's troll-ass move, this could throw the entire Draconian Faction into disarray."

Kali snapped her own sickle tail in time with Dragor in a show of solidarity for the Fire-Breather.

King Jarvok and Lieutenant Zion watched their respective dragons. This was a Draconian issue, and they knew better than to interfere.

The dragons bit into the air, establishing boundaries, each one making their point about the match—Dragor stating his disapproval of letting Famina fight as a viable mating female and Raycor feeling it was her right to enter and noting that Famina had given her word to her Fae rider. They charged, locking horns, the sound like two mountains colliding. Dragor drove Raycor backward, but as they were snout to snout, Raycor did not spit acid; she did something much more practical. "So, if Famina is injured, my chief, she is deemed useless—her main royal acid vesicle destroyed. Will you condemn her to the Spark of Life?" Raycor asked, speaking in their native Draconian language.

Dragor paused his forward charge, and many of the Draconians gasped.

Usually the Draconians spoke in a language the Fae understood, but by reverting back to their ancient tongue, Raycor was making a point, reminding her chief where they came from and why they had left the old ways behind.

Kali translated for her rider, and Jennara covered her mouth in reflex at Raycor's remark. Every Fae knew

Acid vs. Fire or Love vs. Manipulation

Dragor was sentenced to be thrown into the Spark of Life by his father, Chief Peandro, the same day as Los. It was a sore spot for Dragor.

The Fire-Breather lifted his head, unlocking his horns from Raycor, his fire plating compressing. There was a click of his back teeth, and Raycor hunched over, ready to take her punishment. Dragor unleashed his magenta fire skyward instead, along with a deafening roar of anguish and unrelenting scorn. The sky lit up in shades of purples and pinks, the clouds reflecting the fire like water.

When his fire was finished, he dropped his head, his body shaking. Dragor's amber-rimmed eyes stared at Raycor, and his blackened tongue licked his lips. "Never would I do such a thing, Raycor. Famina is not useless. She is kin, always and forever. She is Draconian. I am sorry if you or any of the Draconians even thought I would. None of us are useless. We adapt. I did not want her to fight. I was afraid of losing more after the Massacre of Secor Valley, but you are correct: it was her choice, and now we adapt. Thank you for reminding me." The leader bowed his head to the Acid-Breather, his deep purplish-blue feathers drooping as the last remaining particles of dust settled upon them.

Raycor bowed back. "I, too, must apologize. You would never go back on your word, my chief. We all know that. I was harsh with my language. I am loyal to my kin and my chief. I wanted to remind you of Famina's allegiance to her rider, that is all. As Draconians, our word is our essence."

Dragor snapped his tail. "You are wise, Raycor. We have delayed the Dark Fae long enough. We must step aside so they may continue."

Both dragons locked their gazes upon Kali and Jennara.

"Crisis averted," Jennara whispered, "but I think it's our turn, Kali. No time for strategy planning. Let's go and kick some ass."

Kali let out a roar.

Chapter Seven:
Game On

Jennara marched back to the ring, Kali next to her, their armor soaking up the rays of the sun. Kali's sickle tail swished side to side, making an S pattern in the dirt behind them. Jennara pulled her helmet on. "Kali, you know what needs to be done."

The Fire-Breather snapped her tail, but her gaze remained focused on the arena.

The two competitors stopped at the edge of the ring, watching a group of Fae clean up the remnants of Haus and Famina's match. A wheelbarrow with a pile of what looked like dissolving rock, tree branches, and whatever else was used to scrub the ring went past them in an oozing, bubbling mess. The stench caught in Jennara's throat; she put her hand to her nose. "Oh my."

Kali shook her head a few times and grumbled.

"Okay, okay, try and look tough. Us whining about the smell of dissolved crap isn't exactly going to intimidate Grina and Tatcha."

Kali nodded and the two straightened, both still looking a little green. The dragon started to dry-heave, her black tongue flopping in and out of her mouth as her eyes bulged.

"Don't do it, Kali. If you go, I will."

The dragon puffed out her cheeks, fighting the bile down. Jennara started with short, quick inhales through her mouth.

Azrael observed from the side, muttering aloud at his nominee, "Oh, that's great, Jennara. Something smells bad and that is going to make you and Kali toss your breakfast? Fabulous. They haven't even been called into the ring." He hit his forehead with his palm and slid it down his face. Now Jennara had her hands on her knees as she tried to regain her composure. "Can someone get her water, please!" he called out. Since they hadn't started, he was still within his rights to get his nominee water.

Yagora sauntered up to him and bumped into his shoulder, whispering in his ear, "Gee, Jennara is looking a wee bit sick. Told you she couldn't handle the pressure."

Azrael didn't turn to look at Yagora, keeping his focus on Jennara as she was brought a bucket for Kali and a cup of water. Jennara's color was already getting better, less pale, and her breathing was deeper, more even. *Good.* "She is fine, Yagora. I know you pushed Haus into using a flashbang and told Pria about it, so Grina was prepped. That is cheating. Pria wanted to get rid of Haus because she believed him to be the real threat in the competition. What I don't understand is why you went along with it. He was your nominee." Azrael turned to face his fellow High Council Guard.

Game On

Yagora did not step back, but her eye twitched—always her giveaway.

"Did Haus tell you that?" she spat out.

Azrael gave her a sly smile. "No, Haus told me nothing of the kind." *Technically, Haus told Jennara, not me—partial truth.*

Yagora narrowed her gaze, tucking her hair behind her ear, and tilted her head. "You are making up stories because Haus was originally your nominee, and he lost."

Azrael closed the distance. "Ah, but he is no longer mine." He pointed to Jennara. "She is, and if anything happens to her or Kali that I deem outside the rules of this tournament—well, dear Yagora, I will seek retribution. With or without Jarvok's blessing. Never forget who the right hand of Archangel Michael was for so long." Azrael patted her cheek and walked to the edge of the ring. He looked back to wink at Yagora and saw her swallow hard. *Good.*

Zion took to the platform. "Competitors, take your places. This will decide who goes to the final round!"

The crowd cheered as Grina and Tatcha entered the ring, followed by Jennara and Kali. Acid-Breather and Fire-Breather banners flapped in the breeze. Since this was the third semifinal round, DaVita herself placed the competitors' eggs on each stand. She nodded to Zion, her pastel-tipped hair waving in the wind as she mounted her Ice-Breather, Jasper, and rode out of the ring.

Asa asked all four competitors to meet at the boundary line. "We had a tragedy in our last match; we will not repeat it. I want a clean bout. Do we understand each other?"

The riders and dragons all answered with a resounding, "Yes, Lieutenant."

Grina looked Jennara up and down, smirking. "This won't take long, Tati. Don't worry about backing up. Hold the line," she said, not bothering to lower her voice.

Kali let out a rumble, her fire plating beginning to compress with her breathing.

Asa glanced side to side. "Can you save the trash-talking until after I leave the ring?" She signaled to Zion as she walked away.

"Take your places," Zion commanded.

Tatcha did not move back to guard the egg.

Jennara raised an eyebrow at Grina. *Fine, underestimate us. It's your mistake.* "Kali, guard the egg. They plan on bum-rushing us." Kali backed up, her eyes focused on the threats in front of her.

"Oh, how cute, Tati. They think they are going to put up a fight." Grina cocked her head, smoothing her pink mohawk as she put on her helmet; it complemented the blush-colored Acid-Breather, who tittered in response.

"Fight!" Zion yelled.

Grina and Tatcha bucked and stuttered at the boundary line, but Jennara remained stationary, not falling for their feints. "Steady, Kali," she called back to the Fire-Breather.

Tatcha jumped onto the boulder formation and took to the air as Grina formed a plasma orb. Tatcha spit royal acid and Grina threw the half-formed white orb skyward, catching the acid like a fish in a net, and when the orb came down, Grina roundhouse-kicked it. The plasma ball screamed across the boundary line, just seconds after Grina had formed it.

Jennara jumped to the left to avoid the hit, but the orb caught her left leg.

Game On

"Dynamic energy play," Zion called. "Hit for Grina and Tatcha." The Acid side of Jennara and Kali's egg lit up.

The acid spread up Jennara's leg, eating at her leg greaves, creating channels inside the black kyanite armor. The acid did not eat through the leg armor but compromised its integrity. "Damn it to Lucifer," she muttered, a curse the Dark Fae rarely used. Kali started to run to her, but Jennara held her hand up. "I am okay, girl. Stay. That's what they want. It didn't hit the pants." Flashes of Haus' injuries flew through Jennara's mind.

Grina high-fived the tip of Tatcha's tail as the dragon landed. The crowd chanted, "Acid Assault!" and stomped their feet.

Jennara looked up through her eyelashes at the two. *Our turn.*

"Kali, scorpion sting," she growled through gritted teeth.

The click of Kali's back teeth could be heard. Jennara formed three small plasma orbs, and the dragon flicked three flint rocks over her head with her tail and heated the rocks with her fire breath. Jennara caught them in the plasma orbs, and suddenly the Dark Fae bent down into a standing split and launched each plasma ball one after the other with a kick, the red-hot rocks arcing like a scorpion's tail over her head at Grina and Tatcha. The smaller orbs flew faster than Grina's big one, and all three found their targets. Grina and Tatcha were still busy acting overconfident, huddled together.

"Three direct hits for Jennara and Kali," Zion bellowed.

The Fire side of Grina and Tatcha's egg opened.

"One side is open," Asa announced.

Grina's eyes flashed with rage, her upper lip curling in a snarl.

The onlookers loved it, and the chant of "Blaze Battalion" grew.

"That trick won't work again," Jennara said, backing up. As Kali nodded in agreement, Jennara added, "And I think they are pretty pissed off. So now what?"

The dragon gurgled.

"Stay alive? That's your best idea, Kali?"

Plasma orbs whizzed by, but Kali and Jennara dodged them, both backing up to the egg stand.

"Let's recap: the boundary line stays because they got the first hit within the allotted time. That takes away their ability to ambush us, but they can still rush the line. We have to get another triple play—"

Kali chuckled.

"All right, all right. Repeating a triple play is unlikely. We still have a trick or two."

Grina and Tatcha came right up to the boundary line but did not bother to shield. "That was a lucky hit, Jenna," she taunted.

"Only my friends call me Jenna, and we aren't friends," Jennara shouted back.

Grina mocked wiping a tear from her eye. "Oh, Tati, Jenna said we aren't friends. She hurt my feelings. Guess we will have to hurt something on her."

Tatcha snickered, bolted for the launching boulders, and went skyward as Grina backflipped, throwing plasma orbs for Tatcha to swat with her tail at Jennara and Kali.

Kali took an orb out with her fire, the magenta flames exploding it into firework sparkles that rained downward. The heat generated caused two other orbs to ignite.

The crowd oohed and aahed at the spectacular display of arcing light.

However, Kali needed time to allow her gas bladders to refill, which meant it was up to Jennara to fend off the orbs not incinerated by Kali's fire. She avoided one with ease, but a second orb got through and hit Kali on the side.

"Second hit for Grina and Tatcha," Zion exclaimed as the Acid side of the egg glowed again.

"You good, girl?" Jennara yelled.

The Fire-Breather shook it off and grumbled.

"We can't let them pin us," Jennara said; Kali tittered. "I'm thinking. Give me a second."

Grina sneered. ⬛Let's finish this, Tati. We have toyed with them long enough."

The Acid-Breather jumped off the launching boulders and took to the sky, spitting acid—essentially pinning Jennara and Kali in place, the acid eating away at the ground around the two of them. If the Acid-Breather continued, Jennara and Kali would need to overcome this new obstacle and wouldn't be able to defend their egg. Grina gave a knowing smile and began forming plasma orbs.

Jennara saw her opportunity. "You ready, girl? We are going to try that new armor addition."

Kali put her chest down and her hindquarters up.

"Looks like they are surrendering!" Grina yelled as she threw orbs.

Jennara waited. "Steady." She took one plasma ball hit to the shoulder. As the ground fell away around them. *I need to time this just right before it's too late.*

"Acid side is open," Asa announced.

"Stay, Kali." As Tatcha opened her wings, exposing her belly, Jennara smirked. "Now!"

Kali took two spinning steps and released three boomerangs from her sickle tail, which she had hidden in plain sight. The boomerangs blended seamlessly to the shape of her sickle tail. Jennara formed plasma orbs to ride the tail of the boomerangs. The first one hit Tatcha on its way out, while the other two went past.

"One hit, Jennara and Kali," Asa proclaimed.

The Ice side of Grina and Tatcha's egg glowed, denoting the hit.

"Nice trick, but you missed," Grina said with a curl of her upper lip. But just as the words left her mouth, the second boomerang came around and hit her in the back of the knees, buckling her as the third hit Tatcha in the back of her head, propelled by Jennara's orbs. The dragon's head jerked forward as she fell from the sky to the ground. Grina limped over to Tatcha. The dragon shook her head, stunned.

"Ice side is open," Asa yelled above the astounded crowd.

"Well, I'll be damned." Azrael glanced around, clapping.

Jennara and Kali followed up with more plasma orbs full of fire aimed at the Acid-Breather and Grina.

Grina dove and avoided an orb, but another hit her on the arm. "Tati, get it together. I am not losing to her."

Tatcha was still dazed, lumbering side to side as she tried to stand. The Acid-Breather spit acid to regulate her balance, but it went in every direction but straight.

"Acid side registers a hit for Jennara and Kali."

Kali snorted, but Jennara paused her plasma orb formation. The blush-colored dragon's eyes were vacant. Tatcha couldn't stand straight. *Grina isn't looking after her dragon.* "Kali, Tatcha is hurt. She can't fight. What do we do?"

Grina yelled at Jennara, "You are soft just like they say. You can't even finish the fight. I don't need a dragon to beat you."

Game On

Jennara glanced at Kali. "Guard the egg and back up. Cover me in case Tatcha recovers, and this is a ruse. It's Grina and me now."

Kali chortled. Tatcha had taken out the launching boulder when she tried to walk, and now she was lying down. She wasn't getting up anytime soon. Grina hadn't put any armor on the back of the dragon's head—a careless error.

"Come with it, Grina. Kali will stay back. Tatcha is hurt, and you don't seem to care. You don't deserve to represent any Fae on the elite forces."

The crowd gasped at the insult.

Grina stood, her arms circling at her middle as she gathered her energy, the air popping and sizzling, sparks shooting from her hands. Her face contorted in malice.

Jennara braced for the onslaught. Grina was acting emotionally, her orb charged with anger and rage. They were taught in the ranks to fight without ego. Passion and loyalty differed from arrogance. When an orb was charged with emotion, it could be unstable, and Grina was putting every bit of rage into that sphere.

"Grina, stop! The orb is volatile," Jennara warned. Branches of energy leaked from the glowing globe.

"You would like that!" With a primal scream, Grina poured more anger into the orb, which grew and shuddered, no longer a circle. It was misshapen, with points sticking from it, looking more like a sea urchin than anything else.

Grina's arms shook as the energy coursed over her, her face highlighted by the red and white pulsating light. Her hands worked frantically to keep the throbbing orb from growing any bigger, but she was failing—the sphere was feeding off Grina herself.

"Shut it down, Grina!" Asa commanded. "It will eat your emotions. You are soul-stealing!"

"I can't stop it!" Grina cried out.

Asa removed her gloves and ran for the ring. "I need to drain the extra anger from her."

Jennara hurried to the boundary line to help, but Kali encircled her with her tail and yanked her rider out of the way.

Just as Asa was reaching for Grina, a large blush-colored wing blocked the lieutenant, shielding her as the plasma ball exploded. Asa was thrown back from the blast, but most of the damage was contained on the other side of Tatcha's wing.

The dragon lay on her side and lifted her wing. Grina was unconscious but alive. Kali released Jennara.

"You knew," Jennara whispered to Kali.

The Fire-Breather snorted.

"How?"

Kali clicked and clacked.

"You smelled the change in the ozone. You felt the charge." Jennara hugged her dragon.

In the silence Grina and Tatcha's egg opened, and the crystal dragon flew to King Jarvok.

Grina's armor was decimated, registering the hit.

Jarvok opened his palm as the crystal dragon landed. He closed his gloved fingers around the figurine.

Zion rushed into the ring to help Asa while healers tended to Grina.

"Why did she try for that big of an orb, much less infuse it with rage?" Zion asked as he brushed Asa off, looking for wounds.

"I do not know. Very few of us know that type of orb-forming, and those of us who do know the ramifications." Asa eyed the High Council Guard members suspiciously.

"Will Grina be all right?" Zion inquired.

"After the healers care for her physical wounds, I will look at her emotional status. But not right now. Call the match." Asa stood under her own power, patted him on the shoulder, and glanced at Jennara.

Zion looked toward Jarvok for guidance. The king did not appear happy, but a victory was still a victory—Jennara had won. Jarvok and Dragor both gave a subtle nod.

"Forced hatching. Winner, Jennara and Kali." Zion swallowed after his decree.

Some of the crowd clapped and hollered, but others were not sure how to respond.

Jennara stepped up. "I didn't want to win this way."

"You want to forfeit your victory?" Zion's face scrunched up at such an absurd question.

Azrael was by Jennara's side in a flash. "No, Lieutenant Zion, she does not." He put his hand on Jennara's stomach, pushing her behind him. "She is merely stating the victory feels empty, considering the emotions involved."

Jennara tried to step forward again, but Azrael shot her a death glare.

"Oh, I see." Zion glanced down. "Today's tournament has not gone like any other before. I am sure this is off-putting. The final round will be without incident. Dragor will meditate in solitude while he consults the Sacred Flame and decides on your opponent."

Zion dismissed the crowd until the white smoke from the tower that housed the Sacred Flame turned purple, indicating Dragor had made his decision.

Azrael practically lifted Jennara up by one arm and dragged her out of the ring. "Not a word, Jennara, until we are in private. You too, Kali." The plum-colored Fire-Breather gave a low rumble but followed behind.

Szabo waited for his rider and provided privacy with his wings. Once hidden by the Acid-Breather, Azrael released Jennara with a shove. Kali snarled.

"Hey, that hurt! And why did you interrupt me and Lieutenant Zion? I was—"

"Be quiet, Fae!" Azrael said.

Jennara slammed her mouth shut, the hairs on the back of her neck standing straight up from the power rolling off Azrael.

"You have no idea what you almost did or what is going on. You almost forfeited your victory! Do you understand that? Do you really believe the Draconians would look at Kali with respect, or you, for that matter, because you wanted to win your way? Grina knew what she was doing and messed up. That is her fault." His eyes were lavender fire.

"I wanted to beat her following the rules, and I thought—"

"No, you didn't think. And you did best her. We have been through war, Jennara, and while showing your enemy mercy is one thing, wanting a victory that lives up to your imagination is brainless. Do you even know what Grina was doing or going to do to you?"

Jennara shrugged. "She was making a big plasma ball to take me out."

Azrael removed his helmet and threw it down. "She was soul-stealing, making an orb with nothing but an emotion from deep inside and fusing it with malintent. If it hit you, it would have eaten a piece of your emotional essence, rendering you incapable of aligning your Chakras for some time, maybe even permanently."

"If it was permanent, I would no longer have the ability to form plasma orbs." Her voice trailed off as she looked at Kali. "Our bond would have been broken. Oh, Kali." She hugged the dragon, tears filling her eyes. The dragon dropped her neck to snuggle her rider.

"And considering you aren't an Earthborn Fae, I am thinking this could have…" He glanced away.

"Made me a Weeper." The blood drained from her face with the terrifying realization. She kept her head buried in Kali's neck.

"Yes. Sustaining severe damage to your Chakras—Lieutenant Asa feels this is one of the main factors contributing to a Weeper transformation. No Weeper has a connection to a dragon. Famina is probably what keeps a Fae like Haus from crossing over." He rubbed his eyes.

Jennara sat on the ground, shivers beginning in her legs as the shock set in. Kali moved up behind her, steadying her rider and trying to warm her.

Azrael picked up his helmet and knelt in front of Jennara, tapping her hand with his helmet. She didn't move. He lifted her helmet off and gently placed his index finger under her chin, tipping her head up to meet his eyes. "Jennara, it didn't happen. You aren't a Weeper."

Jennara's eyes were fixed on his. She swallowed. "But—"

Azrael shook his head. "No buts. Tatcha helped save you by shielding Grina, containing the blast. Kali did the rest by pulling you out of range. The Draconians sensed the problem and knew what needed to be done."

Kali snuggled in closer.

"Is Tatcha okay?" Jennara's voice was meek and distant.

"Tatcha will have a pretty bad headache, more from your boomerang than the plasma orb. The dragons' Chakras are different from ours. Asa believes they have an extra one tuned into the Earth's electromagnetic energies. The orb did not affect Tatcha as it would have you." Azrael wiped a tear from her cheek.

"Oh, that's good. What about Grina?" Jennara's voice still sounded hazy.

Azrael exhaled. "I do not know the extent of her injuries, physical or otherwise."

Jennara's gaze grew less disconnected. "I have never heard of soul-stealing. How did Grina know?"

Azrael stood. "That is a much more complicated question. The way to infuse a plasma orb with emotion—that was a well-kept secret in the Brigade. I know you were a newer a recruit when we were abandoned, but even higher up in the ranks, it is not well known. I have a hunch Pria might have known how to do it, but I do not believe she would have taught it to Grina."

"But why? I mean, I get that I pissed off a few Fae, but I'm not hated. This is a big jump. It's like bringing an Elestial Blade to chop vegetables for soup."

Azrael examined his reflection in his helmet, like he was searching for the answers. "I am not sure this is about you personally, Jennara."

"I was almost Weeperized, and you don't think it's personal?" she spat out.

Game On

Azrael put his hand up. "Hear me out. I think there are other elements at play. Haus was set up too—for whatever reason, no one saw you and Kali as a real threat. They wanted you to fight Grina and Tatcha because they believed it would be an easier victory. I think you proved yourself, and Grina reached for a weapon beyond her control in one last act of desperation. I will do some digging. For now, rest up. Dragor has gone to the tower to contemplate your opponent for the final round. We don't know how long he will be, so take the reprieve now while you can get it."

Jennara dusted herself off and tucked her helmet underneath her arm. Szabo lifted his wing for her and Kali to exit. "Thank you, Azrael."

Azrael nodded.

Szabo turned and faced his rider, a chirp escaping him. "Yes, my friend. I am eager to find Yagora, too."

Chapter Eight:
Choices

It was almost dusk, the setting blood sun sending ribbons of red across the sky like a blood-soaked battlefield, fitting for the day. Szabo and Azrael pushed through the throngs of Fae as preparations for the final round took place. Fire-Breather banners were being hung, along with flags of magenta and white. Los flew overhead, holding a long piece of gold silk in his front claws. He perched atop a quartz crystal obelisk and draped the fabric to cover it. The obelisk was inscribed with the names of all Blaze Battalion members. Later tonight, the Battalion might be adding Jennara and Kali to the list, but until the fight was settled, the obelisk would remain covered.

The small amber dragon took off from the obelisk and picked up two wooden planks bearing Jennara's and Kali's names and the Fire sigil. The dragon pranced across the top of the bracket board, playing to the crowd, Los's pink tongue lolling out of his mouth as he danced, shaking his tail with the name planks.

Choices

Fae cheered as Los finally placed Jennara's and Kali's names on the board. Their opponents' bracket lay empty for now. Fire pits roared to life in celebration of a Fire-Breather making it to the final round.

"Besides Jennara's issues with Haus, she is generally respected and liked. Something is off, Szabo," Azrael muttered. The dragon snorted in response. Ahead in the crowd, Azrael glimpsed Yagora, her black-and-white hair standing out in the sea of helmets. "She was always vain about wearing her helmet." Azrael followed her; his gut told him she was at the heart of this.

Yagora walked toward Blood Haven's border wall before dipping out of sight.

"Great, I lost her." Azrael looked around, noticing he and Szabo were far from the fanfare of the tournament.

Only, he hadn't lost her; Yagora came right up behind him and tapped Azrael on the shoulder. "Why are you following me, Azrael?"

Szabo let out a low rumble from the back of his throat at Yagora's stealthy appearance. But then Onichi, Yagora's red Ice-Breather, landed, spreading her wings out and stomping in front of Szabo. Her triangular blue crystalline back scales glittered in the fading light with each gesticulation of her neck. Vapor plumes rose from the dragon's cartilage tusks in a show of dominance and protectiveness.

"I want to talk, Yagora."

"So, talk," Yagora replied, but Onichi did not move, and Szabo began to stalk around the Ice-Breather.

"Tell Onichi to stand down. Szabo is sensing the tension."

Acid leaked from Szabo's canines, a sign the dragon was feeling the situation might not be friendly.

"I didn't do anything," Yagora said.

Azrael put his hands up. "I want to talk. That's all. Now, please, the dragons have had enough excitement today between Famina's injuries, Raycor and Dragor almost fighting. They are sensitive."

Yagora patted her dragon, whispering something Azrael couldn't hear. The dragon bowed her head.

Azrael nodded to Szabo, who folded his wings and sat. "Yagora, I want to know what happened out there. I understand you may have issues with Jennara, but you do realize what Grina could have done, don't you? Please tell me this was all a mistake."

Yagora covered her mouth and nose with her hands, shaking her head. She rubbed at her eyes and dropped her hands. "I didn't teach Grina the soul-stealing orb. She watched me and Pria during our own practices. I never thought she would attempt it. This plan, it's just—"

"What plan? It is just what? Please, I am trying to help."

For a second Azrael thought he had gotten through, that maybe Yagora was still the Angel he had known so long ago, but with each passing moment his hope disintegrated like the ground underneath Szabo's dripping acid.

"Do you know only fifty Ice-Breathers have won the tournament?" she said. "Obendia was the first. An Ice-Breather hasn't won in ten cycles, not including the times a nominee has lost in the final round. Acid-Breather nominees are the strongest candidates, usually winning two to one. The Acid Assault is two hundred strong, followed by the Blaze Battalion at one hundred and twenty-five members."

Azrael pulled at his ponytail. "What does this have to do with anything?"

Choices

"Because when King Jarvok leaves to go play house with the Light Fae Queen, if he takes Zion and Raycor, that leaves the commander spot open for the Acid Assault—and whoever commands that will most likely lead Blood Haven. If he leaves Zion, and the Acid Assault gains another dragon—"

Azrael smacked his forehead. "If the Acid Assault gained another dragon loyal to Pria, you thought this would put her in contention to lead the Acid Assault and be named Jarvok's successor to Blood Haven if Zion goes. Even if Zion stays, Pria could move into the number-two position if she has loyalty from the Acid-Breathers by placing one of theirs on the Assault. But what about Asa?"

Yagora laughed. "Please, she is of no concern or threat to us. Jarvok isn't even going to consider her. It took Yanka three cycles to win. Imagine that—our almighty third-in-command didn't win her first time out. Even Onichi won the first time. Pria would fight tooth and nail before she let that happen."

"I see what Pria gains from this, but what about you?"

"Pria promised I would become her second-in-command."

"What about me, Ezekiel, or Johan? You don't believe we are worthy of Jarvok's consideration?"

Yagora shrugged. "You are the only one of us who can imbue Fae with Elestial Blades. You are too much of a commodity to rule. You have always been protected. As for Johan or Zeke, well, Johan is lazy, and Zeke—let's just say Zeke will show his weaknesses one way or another. Pria is best suited. She is ruthless and cunning. Zion is a troll's prick who happened to get to Jarvok first, that's all. I am tired of bowing down to Fae who aren't worthy."

"Pria is something, all right. So you planned this. Have you been stacking the deck this entire time?"

Yagora shrugged.

"Now that Jennara is in the finals, what happens?"

"Nothing. She will lose, no dragon will be added to the ranks, and we will have to figure out a new course of action. If anything, it looks worse on you for backing her and better on me because I knew she wasn't ready." Yagora was nonchalant in her explanation.

"You did this. Haus lost his eye, Famina might not be able to spawn, and we don't yet know the extent of Grina's damage. Jennara could have lost her bond with Kali and been sent down the road of a Weeper because you think Pria is a better leader than Zion? And you want to be her second-in-command. I mean, screw the rest of the High Council Guard and the lives you have destroyed. If Dragor and Raycor weren't more civilized than you, those two could have killed each other because you don't like Zion?" Azrael could feel how big his eyes were.

"I never said I didn't like Zion. I said he shouldn't be Jarvok's successor." She gave him a deadpan stare.

"You think it should be Pria? A lazy, two-faced shrill of a Fae who made you do all her dirty work and promised to make you second banana? So she could rule, take the credit, and have you do all the work. You two deserve each other." He threw his hands up, the disappointment evident.

Yagora snarled and ran up to him, Onichi growling. "How dare you pass judgment!"

Azrael unsheathed his Elestial Blade and pointed it at Yagora, who slid to a stop. "I do not judge. Choose your next move carefully, Yagora Devaroux. Yes, I have known you long enough to remember your full birth name."

Choices

Yagora held her chin up; Azrael's blade was inches from her throat. His nostrils flared. "I nominated Jennara, and you put her in danger for a power grab to satisfy Pria. Not merely physical danger but a level of peril I cannot fathom. I should take your head."

Yagora swallowed. "Are you going to tell King Jarvok?"

Azrael sheathed his blade with a flick of his wrist, and the light receded along with the Auric weapon as it was reabsorbed into his forearm. "I should, but no. I have no proof. You and Pria would lie. For two seconds, I thought you felt some remorse." He paced, shaking his head. "But it was fleeting, maybe all for show. I feel sorry for you, Yagora—you aren't even worthy of my blade. Keep following Pria around like a lost troll looking for their next fix of snow pollen. She plays you, and you let her. You will eventually cross a line you can't come back from. Someone or something will be the tool of your karma."

Yagora rushed Azrael, who sidestepped and used her momentum to send her tumbling. "You mistake kindness for weakness. That was always your problem."

Yagora picked up a rock and threw it at Azrael; he dodged it easily. She yelled in frustration.

He bent down to look her in the eyes. Yagora was breathing frenetically, her hair falling in her face as her shoulders moved up and down. She flinched when Azrael slid her bangs out of her way. "I think you do love Pria, or else you would not be this upset, but love should be a two-way street or else it is obsession. Stop trying to earn her affection."

Yagora looked into the distance and changed the subject in a futile attempt to hurt or distract Azrael. "What happens when Jennara loses?"

Azrael rose. "She won't. I have faith in Jennara and Kali. They will win this tournament."

Yagora stayed on the ground. "Why do you have faith in them?" Disgust dripped from her words, but he knew it was more envy than anything else.

A soft smile grazed his lips. "Because they both have heart. I will take a Fae with heart over natural talent any day. Skills can be taught—heart can't. Just ask Pria." Before Yagora could answer, Azrael looked up at the smoke billowing from the tower; it was turning from light purple to violet, similar to spring crocuses emerging from winter's final snowfall. "Dragor has reached his decision. Come, Szabo."

Yagora called after him, "I told you I was a horrible Fae, Azrael. I told you!"

Azrael mounted his dragon, glancing over his shoulder at her. "Yes, you did. Actually, you said 'terrible,' and I think you might have been telling the truth. I should have listened, but I am not good at noticing social cues. I have spent too much time in my forge, remember?"

Szabo snorted in agreement, and the two departed.

Chapter Nine:
Opponent

Torches burned, their light casting exaggerated shadows on the side of the stone coliseum entrance. The flames seemed alive with anticipation that a Fire-Breather would be fighting tonight, as if every incarnation of fire was aware of the honor Kali carried on her fire plating. When Szabo and Azrael touched down at the edge of the coliseum, Fae were filing in. The scent of sage and cedar filled the air, and Azrael inhaled the earthy aroma. They had lit the sage to cleanse the ring.

The energy was palpable; everyone wanted to know whom Jennara and Kali would face in the final round. Azrael scanned the sea of Fae for his nominee, wanting to give her a pep talk, but she was nowhere to be found. "Must be inside already," he told Szabo. Azrael did spot Pria leaning on a column, looking unbothered. "Figures, the puppet master seems unconcerned with the problems she has caused."

Fire, Ice, Acid, and Heart

As if she sensed Azrael's eyes on her, Pria brushed her wavy teal hair from her face and blew him a kiss, then pushed off the column and walked inside.

"The nerve," he mumbled to Szabo. "I swear Pria was not born with a heart or a conscience. How Zion could have ever aura-blended with that vile creature is beyond me."

"Zion would aura-blend with a tree if the hole was low enough." Lieutenant Asa stood next to him, arms folded, hip cocked to the side; even her mask could not hide her knowing smirk. "So, besides Zion's poor taste in aura-blending partners, what has Pria done now?"

Azrael dropped his head. "What hasn't she done is a better question, Lieutenant, but nothing I can prove. How is Grina?"

Asa frowned. "That was a cryptic answer. Does this have something to do with Grina's soul-sucking attempt?"

"I don't know. Yes. No." Azrael raised his head. "Grina acted of her own accord. If I say anything without proof, it will seem like I am blaming Pria because my nominee almost got hurt. For the record, Jennara is fine. I will look like a complainer, overprotective, and like I am giving Jennara special treatment, which will feed into the rumors Jennara aura-blended with me to be nominated. So, I cannot say a word." He took a long inhale and exhale to calm himself.

Asa smoothed her hair, raking her fingers through her ponytail. "Well, it seems you have it all figured out." Her tone was flat.

Azrael slapped the sides of his legs. "What do you want me to say? I tried to help a Fae who deserved a chance, and I nearly got her turned down the path of a Weeper. Haus lost an eye, Famina may not be able to spawn, and

Opponent

Grina—you never answered my question on how she is. This is all because I had to act magnanimously. Next time I'll stay in my forge." He sank to the ground.

Asa nodded along, licking her lips. "Are you done?"

"Excuse me?"

Asa crouched down, balancing on the balls of her feet. "Are you done feeling sorry for yourself? It's unbecoming."

Azrael rested his cheek on one hand, elbow on his knee. "I do not feel sorry for myself. I was the right hand of Arch—"

"Blah, blah, Archangel Michael—I have heard your title for centuries, Azrael. If you could print it on a sash and wear it, I think you would."

Azrael jerked his head back.

Asa made a circular motion with her finger. "Oh, and this *is* a pity party if I ever saw one. You have a nominee ready to face Dragor's choice, and you are supposed to be standing with her in the ring when she finds out who it is. Get up off your ass and go to her. Stop blaming yourself. None of this is your fault. I know Pria had something to do with it, and Yagora, but like you so eloquently pointed out, we have no proof. So, quit your bitching and get out there. Don't let them win by letting Jennara down."

Azrael's lavender eyes were wide. "First of all, I wouldn't wear a sash."

Asa put a palm up. "I am an empath, so let's skip this debate and get on with it."

Azrael nodded. "But if you know Pria and Yagora are behind this, why not go to the king? Since you *are* an empath." He realized he sounded like Jennara and their past conversations. *Maybe I have been hanging around*

Jennara and Kali too much. Next I'll start asking Szabo to snap a sickle tail every time he agrees with me. Geez.

"Pria and Yagora are cold and calculating and cover their tracks well. And I can't go using my abilities and poking around like that—it's against Jarvok's rules." Asa flushed; the last time she had explored others' emotions, she had almost gotten herself thrown in the Pit.

Azrael opened his mouth to protest, but Asa went on, "Imagine if I went around busting into every Fae's aura someone had suspicions about. Pria and Yagora would have led the revolt against me a long time ago. Anytime a Fae was unhappy with Jarvok, the feeling could be seen as treason."

Azrael rubbed his temples. "But we have more than suspicions about Yagora and Pria. Can't you..." He waved his hands. "You know, do your thing."

Asa looked at him through her lashes and waved her hands back at him. "My *thing*? Either that was an attempt at a joke, or you really are that socially awkward. No, I can't, not even to Pria and Yagora. It would be wrong. Sometimes I think those two will be the death of me."

Azrael winced at her expression.

"I see it like this: yes, you want justice for what those two troll's pricks are doing, but you are more upset that you care for someone. And you, my Fae friend, have not let yourself care for any Fae in, well ... I can't even remember. Your walls are built higher than this fortress." She placed a gentle hand on his knee. "That isn't a judgment. As Michael's right hand, you were taught to detach, not to care. How else would you be able to implant Elestial Blades in your fellow Power Brigade members?"

Opponent

Azrael tilted his head, contemplating her rationale. "Yagora said something similar but not as powerfully or helpfully. She meant it to be an insult, to wound. What you are saying makes sense. I do care for Jennara like a baby dragon. Is that odd? I am so awkward with social norms."

Asa gave him a soft smile. "We have established your awkwardness. It's part of your charm, and no, my friend, what you are feeling for Jennara and Kali, that protectiveness, is not odd. Do not let Yagora and Pria rob you of this. Even the guilt and the uncomfortable feelings are all part of living as Fae, our experience. Now go to your nominee and stand with her in the circle. Be proud with her. Regardless of what happens today, you backed the right dragon."

He stood. "Thank you, Lieutenant."

"Chaos be with you and your nominees."

Asa and Azrael grabbed forearms on their Elestial Blade side in a sign of respect.

"And with you." Azrael smiled. He took off running toward the arena, Szabo galloping behind him.

Asa watched after him, relieved he had not asked again about Grina. Asa's diagnosis of Grina's Chakras had revealed the Fae would be a Weeper by the new moon, when all seven of her Chakras would be completely out of balance, no longer able to spin and beyond saving. Grina had asked to be sent to her Oblivion before that happened. But that was for Jarvok to decide and ultimately follow through with. *I would love to catch Yagora or Pria in something, and one day I will, by all that is light in the universe. They will pay dearly for this.*

Chapter Ten:
Heart

Jennara and Kali waited at the foot of the platform. Cauldron fires blazed near them to honor the Fire-Breather making it to the final round. The sky held the last remnants of light while a few early stars winked in as if they were curious about the event. King Jarvok sat in his makeshift throne, Lieutenant Zion standing to his right and the High Council Guard members to the left. The leaders of the Acid Assault, the Ice Invaders, and the Blaze Battalion remained on their respective perches. Dragor circled above, waiting until all Fae and dragons were present before making his announcement.

Lieutenant Asa was unaccounted for, but more concerning was the absence of High Council Guard Azrael, Jennara's sponsor. Per the rules of the tournament, both the nominee and their sponsor were to be present to hear Dragor's choice of final combatants.

Another few minutes passed and Jennara began shuffling her feet, kicking at the ground. Kali picked up on her rider's anxiety and compressed her fire plating rhythmically.

Heart

Jennara leaned over, keeping her eyes on the raised area. "Do you think Azrael bailed on us, girl?"

The dragon snorted, as though to say, "Looks that way."

"Troll's balls."

A screech was heard from above; Dragor was growing impatient with the delay.

Asa slipped onto the platform, her hand on Zion's shoulder. "My apologies," she whispered as she took her place. She shot Pria and Yagora an icy glare, but the Fae crowding the coliseum were far too distracted by a new silhouette stepping into the ring. The Fae had a limp and was too tall to be Azrael.

As the figure entered from the back, the distinct sound of tiny skulls clattering together could be heard as he approached the two nominees. Kali nudged Jennara's side.

"Hausman, what is the meaning of this?" King Jarvok bellowed.

Jennara was astonished at Haus' appearance. The compresses were barely hanging from his wounds, and the eye patch was stained with dried blue blood. But Haus straightened as the king called his name. He bent to one knee, grimacing in pain. "My liege, High Council Guard Azrael is not present, and he is my commander. Therefore I humbly ask to step in and support Jennara in his absence."

"What are you doing, Fae?" Jennara mumbled to Haus, fighting not to look at him. "You are injured—and by the way, you hate us." She motioned between herself and Kali.

Kali snapped her tail.

Haus gave a low chuckle. "I don't hate you, Jennara, or Kali." His good eye slid up to her. "I might not like you, but damn, I respect you. Besides, I enjoy winning too much not to be part of a winning team." He smirked. "There were whispers by the healers that Commander Azrael had not shown for you. I couldn't let that happen, you know, for the honor of my platoon. I would wink but that seems redundant." Haus pointed to his eye and Jennara shook her head, not sure if it was okay to laugh. Kali rolled her eyes.

"That won't be necessary, Hausman," a voice called from the side. Azrael jogged in.

Asa exhaled in relief.

"You are excused, Hausman, but thank you. Please return to the healer's tents," Jarvok commanded.

Azrael helped Haus up. "Win, Jennara," the injured Fae said. "Prove them wrong just like you proved me. Chaos be with you."

Two healers staggered forward, holding their sides.

"Well, hello there," he said. "I see you finally found me."

The healers didn't look happy, and Jennara couldn't help but laugh at his commentary as tears rolled down her cheeks. "He beat up his healers to come stand by my side," she whispered, shaking her head.

"It would appear so. There might be hope for Haus after all," Azrael said, trying to stifle his own amusement.

Dragor roared, and the Fae returned their attention to the platform.

"Azrael, how nice of you to join us. I sincerely hope I did not interrupt your day," King Jarvok said.

Azrael bent his knee. "Please forgive me, my liege. I have never had a nominee make it to the final round, and Lieutenant Asa was explaining to me the duties of a sponsor."

"If you are well versed in your commitments, can we get on with this?"

"Yes, my liege." Azrael stood and stepped back in line with Jennara.

"You had us worried," Jennara mumbled.

"I do apologize. Forgive me," Azrael said as they watched Dragor circle and land.

The Draconian leader's wings kicked up dust particles, which glittered in the firelight. Dragor stood silent and majestic in the last rays of the blood sun as it sank below the horizon, not to be seen again until next year, when this cycle would repeat itself.

Jennara leaned over. "What happens now?"

"I'll be damned if I know," Azrael replied.

She did a double-take. "I thought Asa was briefing you?"

"Not on Dragor. Each tournament, he does things differently. We never know what he is going to do." Azrael shrugged.

Jennara smacked her forehead with her palm and her hand slid down her face, a very Azrael mannerism. "Troll's balls."

Kali glanced between the Fae; she didn't seem too concerned about whatever her chief was going to do. Her gold-and-navy-tipped feathers blew in the early evening's breeze. She was the picture of serenity.

Dragor stomped his front leg, and Los flew to the wooden board that was covered in the Fire-Breathers' banner.

"Here we go," Azrael spoke under his breath.

Dragor roared, and Los drew back the banner, revealing Jennara and Kali's bracket: they would be facing off against Ezekiel and his Fire-Breather, Construct.

"By all that is light in the universe," Jennara whispered.

"You can say that again." Azrael's eyes were wide.

Kali snapped her sickle tail, ready to fight.

Dragor's neck snaked from the board to the competitors.

King Jarvok made the match official: "Jennara and Kali will meet Ezekiel and, from the Eastern region of the Impolita Valley, Construct, in the final round. DaVita, please present their eggs."

DaVita rode Jasper into the ring; gold, green, magenta, and white silk ribbons were attached to Jasper's tail in honor of the final match. A cross-body pouch held Jennara's and Ezekiel's eggs. She placed them each on their respective holders. Ezekiel's egg was more battle worn as it was the original egg from the first-ever winner of the tournament. Each defender had protected this egg in the tournaments since. If Jennara and Kali won, their egg would be sealed and never used again.

DaVita and Jasper both paid respects to Jarvok and Dragor, and then she turned to Jennara. "Chaos be with you," she said, dropping a small tan-and-dark-brown-striped crystal at Jennara's feet. Kali sniffed at the crystal. It was a tiger's-eye crystal, known for good luck in competition; it promoted healing and protection. Jennara rolled the smooth, cool stone in her hand. "Thank you," she said, but DaVita and Jasper were already on the platform at the king's side.

The moment of peace was broken by a roar from above, followed by an outbreak of fire from the Blaze Battalion. Construct and Ezekiel flew in, landing to the right of Jennara, Kali, and Azrael.

Construct's body was half black with age, but his wings had retained their bright lemon-yellow coloring. His eyes, the irises rimmed in royal blue, scanned his competitors, and he snorted, unimpressed. The matching blue-and-black-tipped feathers around his fire plating waved in the breeze. Construct was deadly and had been one of the first to win this tournament.

Ezekiel hopped off his dragon and stood next to Azrael. "Good to see you, Azrael." His voice was flat; he did not bother with Jennara.

"And you Ezekiel." Azrael stood with his hands behind his back, tall and ready.

Jarvok raised his hands. "Competitors, this tournament has been unusual, but Dragor and I expect an honorable fight. In Dragor's highest wisdom, he has selected you, Ezekiel, and your dragon, Construct, to represent the final test for Jennara and Kali. See you honor him and the Dark Fae. Fight with integrity, perseverance, honor, and indomitable spirit."

"Integrity, perseverance, honor, and indomitable spirit," Jennara, Kali, Ezekiel, and Construct repeated back.

Zion took the lead next. "For the final round, the rules change. First, the ring size doubles to one hundred yards."

Jennara hadn't noticed it before, too busy worrying if Azrael was going to show, but yes, the ring was indeed bigger, much bigger.

Hazards had been added too: more jumping-off rocks, water puddles, and dark pits. Zion explained that their eggs would stay on the stand for the first minute of the round. After one minute, if there were no hits, the boundary line would be erased, and the competitors must carry their eggs with them. The egg could be taken by force but must be returned to the platform for the win. Finally, this round only requires six hits to force a hatching, two per side.

"Azrael, you will have five minutes to strategize with your nominee." Jarvok gestured between Azrael and Jennara.

"Yes, my liege."

"Chaos be with you!" Jarvok raised his arms.

The entire arena replied, "Chaos be with you!"

Ezekiel smirked as he gave Jennara one look up and down. She did not flinch.

But once Ezekiel walked away, she held her stomach like she was going to be sick. "Um, didn't Ezekiel fight side by side with Yagora at the Battle of the Red Sea? Aren't they like best Fae?"

Azrael waved her concern off. "Yes, they did fight at the Red Sea, and no Fae is best anything with Yagora. Ezekiel is a fair Fae. Stop letting them in your head, Jennara."

Kali snapped her tail a few times.

"Are we better letting this go to a game of capture-the-egg or keeping the boundary line?" Jennara asked, getting her game face back on.

"Ezekiel's hand-to-hand combat skills are not as good as Yagora's, but he is still not to be taken lightly. Construct is the threat from a distance. I think it is best we take it to a close range. You and Kali will need to use your smaller stature and your speed and intellect. Get in and get out. Be smart. With the boundary line in place, Construct has the advantage—his fire-breathing is stronger, given his size. We need to try for a no-hit."

Jennara glanced at Kali. "Are you good with this plan, girl?" Kali clicked and clacked her teeth, and Jennara smiled. "I agree we can kick their ass."

"Time is up, Azrael," Zion announced.

Heart

Azrael laid a hand on Jennara's shoulder and one on Kali's side. "You are ready. I believe in you. No matter what happens, I am proud of you both. Chaos be with you."

This was not merely a pep talk; they were ready, and he did believe in them. That was all he had to say.

Jennara smiled, pulling on her helmet. "Thank you." Instead of giving Azrael the Power Angel salute, she hugged him. Azrael stood stiffly, arms at his sides, but his gaze skimmed to Asa on the platform, who smirked. Despite her mask, he could sense the satisfaction on her face.

Azrael clumsily extracted his right arm from Jennara's hug and patted her on her back. "There, there. You are welcome." He sighed, and she released him. Jennara pivoted, but Azrael called her back. "By the way, what are the symbols on Kali's snout armor? What do they mean?"

Jennara yelled, "The top is the sigil for heart and the bottom means home. Kali is my heart, and when I found her, I realized I was home." Jennara pointed to her own heart and then to the dragon. "Heart and home." She ran toward the starting position.

Azrael covered his mouth, trying to hide his smile.

Chapter Eleven:
Rumble in the Ring

The energy in the coliseum was electric. Green banners waved bearing Blaze Battalion sigils, showing loyalty to Construct, while magenta Fire-Breather flags flew for Kali and Jennara. Little Ones in attendance wore paper dragon masks representing their favorite type of dragon and roared as the crowd cheered.

The platform and canopy were decorated with small triangular flags, each one with a sigil symbolizing the champion from the previous tournaments. Jarvok sat at the center of the platform with Zion at the head to act as the first referee, Asa on the ground as a line judge. High Council Guard members Jonah, Pria, and Yagora were stationed on benches to the king's left, with DaVita and Jasper to Jarvok's right—DaVita taking the place of honor for her hard work in fashioning the eggs used in the competition. Los sat near Jasper, ready to be a cheerleader when needed. The crowd loved Los, and the little dragon adored the adulation. Dragor was perched to the right of the platform, watching with his commanders.

Rumble in the Ring

Azrael stood just outside the ring to verbally assist Jennara. He glanced up at Yagora, who met his eyes for a moment, then looked away. Pria, however, stared right down at him, not an ounce of contrition in her gaze. She winked and he snarled. Pria elbowed Yagora and pointed at Azrael, the two Fae giggling like human courtiers, making it clear it was at his expense.

Zion raised his arms. "Competitors, take your places."

Jennara and Kali lined up toward the front of the ring in an attempt to crowd Ezekiel and Construct.

Ezekiel shrugged at his dragon. "Sure, we can play it their way," he grumbled as he closed the distance, placing one boot inches from the line. Ezekiel crouched down, one hand out in a fist, his knees bent. He flexed his other hand and looked up at Jennara through his helmet. Every muscle was poised and ready to spring. Determination and focus permeated the air around him.

She scoffed. To her, Ezekiel was not a High Council Guard member but another competitor. Her hands flexed and relaxed in time with his, and she leaned forward, her front knee bent, shoulders over her hips, ready to attack—like a troll defending their bridge.

Zion looked to Ezekiel, who nodded, and to Jennara, who gave a subtle chin tilt.

The second-in-command dropped his arms, yelling, "Fight!"

Ezekiel was a different caliber of fighter than any Fae Jennara had faced. His plasma ball was formed before Zion's arms had relaxed. It whirled at her and she front-flipped out of the way, barely dodging it.

She took cover behind a launching rock to catch her breath. "Kali, you okay?"

The dragon called back to signal she was safe.

"Come now, Jennara. You are making this too easy," Ezekiel said. "I mean, hiding already? It was only a plasma ball."

"Keep him busy," Azrael reminded her.

Kali swept in, grabbed Jennara, and threw her rider on her back. The two zigzagged as Construct blew streams of fire.

"That's it. Use your speed," Azrael said.

Jennara tried fire caught in plasma balls, but Ezekiel laughed them off.

"Immature tricks, my dear. They may have worked on the others, but for the Blaze Battalion, no."

"Kali, keep moving—harder to hit a moving target," Azrael called.

"No hits," Asa proclaimed.

"Erase the line—competitors, grab your eggs. You must carry them with you," Zion yelled above the cheering crowd. He tossed four black satchels into the middle of the ring.

Ezekiel and Construct only grabbed one of the two bags marked for them.

Jennara and Kali retrieved both their bags and circled back for the egg. "I'll carry it first, and we will toss it between the two of us." Jennara winked at the Fire-Breather and placed a rock in Kali's bag. "Now the fun begins."

Kali and Jennara split up, veering off in different directions. Jennara placed her egg in her bag and slung the bag across her body.

Ezekiel wore his bag across his body too and stayed on Construct as the two flew above the ring. "Critical error, Jennara—I have the higher ground," he called.

"But I also know where your egg is. Are you sure you know where mine is?" she called back.

Ezekiel and Construct paused midair, confused at her remark. Kali flew up behind the two and breathed fire, hitting them in the back.

"One hit for Kali and Jennara," Asa called.

Azrael jumped in the air and cheered.

Jennara rolled out of the way as Construct dove for her.

Kali was smaller and maneuvered more easily than the big dragon. Tucking her wings in close, she took a sharp angle, aiming low, her body tight, and flew just under the yellow Fire-Breather's stomach like an arrowhead. Kali reached her rider first and scooped her out of harm's way with her mouth just in time. They pulled up in a U-shaped aerial maneuver, with Kali tossing Jennara into the air—Jennara backflipped with a "Yippee!" and landed on the Fire-Breather's back. She switched bags with Kali, hiding the action from Ezekiel. "Thanks, girl. Enough playing—let's grab their egg and end this."

Construct and Ezekiel were right behind them. Kali barrel-rolled, but Construct kept up. The two dragons body-checked each other in midair, their massive Kyanite armor creaking with the impact, but these were considered innocuous hits and did not register damage to the eggs. Kali swerved off her path with each knock from the much bigger Fire-Breather. The two dragons snapped in the air when they got close to each other.

Yanka and Asa took to the air to make sure it remained a fair fight, keeping a safe distance as the four competitors flew straight upward, using their claws to battle, much like eagles.

Jennara held tight as Construct's massive front claws dug in on Kali and twisted, sending the dragon into a dive roll she could not control. Ezekiel seized the moment and threw a plasma ball that hit Kali on her side.

"Hit for Ezekiel and Construct," Asa said.

Azrael was searching the darkened sky. Construct's yellow wings were easier to spot than Kali's plum-colored body. "Come on, Jennara. Be smart," he pleaded, Azrael's emotions were getting the best of him. He knew Jennara couldn't hear him.

The force from the plasma ball helped redirect Kali; she used it to straighten out of her spin. "Land, girl," Jennara said. "I have an idea. We will finish them on the ground."

Kali clicked and clacked, and with a flap of her wings, she headed for coverage behind a launching rock formation.

Jennara dismounted and inspected the plasma ball hit on Kali's side, running her hand over the armor. There was an indentation, and it was still hot to the touch. "Wow, Ezekiel isn't messing around. You okay?" The dragon nodded. "Do you need calendula salve?" Kali shook her head. "All our plans to trick them aren't going to work. Ezekiel is too smart and too strong. We are stronger together. Hold the egg, and—"

As they were switching bags, the rock exploded as Construct hit it with fire. Kali and Jennara went careening into the air. Then Jennara felt the hit on her back and heard Asa's call.

"Hit, Ezekiel and Construct. Fire side is open."

Jennara smacked the ground with her palm. "Troll's balls."

"Get up, Jennara!" Azrael shouted. "What are you doing? Get up!"

Rumble in the Ring

Ezekiel readied another plasma ball.

Jennara pulled herself up, her back spasming as she got to her knees. She dropped down again. Kali ran to her, but another plasma ball hit Jennara in the chest, sending her onto her back. She screamed in pain.

"Direct hit, Ezekiel and Construct." Zion called this one.

"Please, Jennara. Fight a little," Ezekiel teased.

Kali was in front of her rider, tail snapping. Jennara stayed crouched and gathered her strength to stand.

Azrael wanted to stop the match—Jennara was hurt badly. But he knew that if he did, she would never get another chance. He needed to have faith in her and Kali.

Construct came up behind Ezekiel, who said to Jennara, "I can take the egg and end this now. You are in pain, and I am not a cruel Fae. Hand it over." He gestured with his hand out, his fingers wiggling.

Kali growled.

"Never" was heard from behind the dragon. "If you want the egg, come and get it, you troll's prick."

Ezekiel glanced over his shoulder at Construct and shrugged. "I kind of respect her for that, but the Fae can't even stand."

Construct snapped his tail back at his rider, saying, "Finish her."

"I agree, buddy. She asked for it." Ezekiel craned his neck, trying to look behind Kali as he spoke to Jennara. "I was just going to take it from you, but now I will humiliate you. That is what it means to be a High Council Guard member and part of the Blaze Battalion. Fire in our hearts and ice in our veins."

"Oh, by all that is light in the universe, you could send me to my Oblivion with all this talk!" She threw a rock at him over Kali; it landed at Ezekiel's feet. "Really? Fire in your heart and ice in your veins. That is the worst thing I have ever heard, Ezekiel! You should have said something like 'We burn our enemies with no remorse.'"

Jennara wasn't just goading Ezekiel, though—she was using this time to stand while Kali blocked their view of her.

"Why, you disrespectful piece of goblin shit, I am going to teach you some manners." Ezekiel threw a plasma ball, but Kali was ready, and as the ball was released, Kali extended a Blue Kyanite staff from her sickle tail, turned sideways, and hit the plasma ball back at Ezekiel. The Fae was stunned by the sight of the dragon wielding a weapon. He did not even try to dodge the ball, taking the hit square in the chest.

Zion looked to DaVita on the platform, who had smaller versions of each of the competitor's eggs since no one could see the originals. She nodded as Ezekiel's egg glowed and the petal cracked open.

"Hit, Jennara and Kali. Fire side open," Zion announced.

Jennara vaulted over Kali and landed on Ezekiel's chest, then grabbed his egg pouch. She was breathing heavily; this had taken all her strength, and her back was giving out. The familiar click of a Fire-Breather's back teeth sounded— Construct was close. Kali stepped between them. Jennara rolled off Ezekiel and grimaced in pain. She still had to get the egg to the platform to present it for a clean takeaway.

"*Run!*" Azrael yelled.

The crowd was on its feet, cheering for their favorite competitors. Chants of "Run, Jennara!" or "Get her!" rang out.

As Construct and Kali squared off, Jennara lay on her back, clutching Ezekiel's satchel to her chest, writhing in pain. He mounted her and the two grappled for control. She managed to get his bag around her, leaving her hands free, but her movement was limited. Jennara bucked a few times, but that only inflamed her pain and didn't do much to move Ezekiel. Their only saving grace was that they were too close to the Fire-Breathers for either dragon to use their oral defense. The dragons were relegated to fighting like the Fae. However, Kali had a weapon and was making the most of it, swinging the Kyanite staff at Construct to keep the larger dragon at bay.

Azrael ran up the sideline, trying to help Jennara by yelling grappling moves, but she was in too much pain. If she attempted a plasma ball this close to blast Ezekiel off her, there was a chance it would bounce back and register a strike against her.

Ezekiel reached for the satchel, but both bags were identical. If he took both back and Zion opened the wrong one first, the victory would be Jennara's. The two Fae twisted and fought for control, which scrambled the satchels more. Frustrated, Ezekiel grabbed Jennara around the throat, and she beat at his arm, trying to break his grip from underneath.

"Give me the satchel with your egg!" He applied more pressure until she slowed her struggling. Ezekiel watched as her green eyes lost focus and her hands, which had been trying to break his grip, hung in the air for a minute frozen, then fell to her side.

"He is going to kill her!" Azrael shouted.

Kali lifted her head and charged at Construct, hitting the dragon across the jaw with the Kyanite staff, knocking the dragon on his ass. Then she skidded and made a

U-turn, heading for her rider. Construct shook his head and blinked, dazed but not out.

Kali had Ezekiel in her sights. The High Council Guard looked into the plum-colored dragon's eyes and released his grip on Jennara, but before Kali could snap at Ezekiel, Construct grabbed her by her sickle tail and yanked her backward and up. Kali watched from the air as Ezekiel grew smaller on the ground, the Kyanite staff beside him and Jennara.

The dragon twisted around to look up. "I should have hit you harder," Kali said to Construct.

"Yes, you should have." Deep laughter emanated from Construct's belly. He peeked over his shoulder and smiled. "I respect you for the attempt, but next time put your hips into it more."

Kali folded her front claws. "Next time," she harrumphed, then said, louder, "I am worried about my rider."

"You should be. Ezekiel is a ferocious Fae, but he won't send her to her Oblivion. He is not like that. Now if you don't mind, it's time we end this. Better luck next year," Construct said.

"What?" But before Kali could get an answer, Construct threw the smaller dragon. She spun like a pinwheel through the air, disoriented, the stars becoming nothing but streaks of light. "I have wings. What am I doing?" The closer her wings were to her body, the faster she spun, but if she extended her wings, she slowed. "Amateur move," she grumbled, chastising herself.

Rumble in the Ring

Jennara was losing, and she knew it. She saw Kali try to get to her, only to have Construct yank her dragon away. Azrael was yelling something, but she couldn't hear him anymore. Jennara focused on Ezekiel, attempting to get her arms to move. Nothing happened. Her gaze drifted as her head lolled to the side for a moment, which was when she saw the Kyanite staff close to her leg. Ezekiel's voice was muffled—he was saying something. The ground shook as Construct landed next to her, taking Ezekiel's attention away from Jennara for a second.

"Did you take care of her dragon?"

Construct clicked and clacked a victorious sound, and Jennara felt her blood go cold.

"Thank you. Let's finish this."

A whistling sound came from above, and Ezekiel held his left hand up to catch Kali's tail boomerang, then the boomerang that followed, tossing them aside. Jennara used the distraction to kick the Kyanite staff up, grab it, and swat at Ezekiel. The sound of Kali's teeth followed, and Construct blocked them as magenta fire came raining down.

"I thought you took care of her?" Ezekiel barked.

Jennara rolled out of the way, using the staff to get to her feet, and limped for cover behind a launching rock while Kali tried to buy her time. She coughed, trying to fill her lungs with air. Then she noticed the water hazard nearby. "Kali!" she cried.

The dragon swooped in for a moment.

"I have a plan," Jennara said, and glanced at the water hazard. "Do you have any boomerangs left?"

Meanwhile Ezekiel was nose to snout with Construct. "I am not losing to a nominee trained by Yagora. Do we understand each other? I have played fourth troll to her for far too long. I can't do this anymore, Construct. We beat them, and we move up in the Guard. I am sure Kali is a fine dragon, but enough. Deal with it."

Azrael shook his head on the sidelines. The High Council Guard had become nothing more than a breeding ground for backstabbing, he realized, and old friends constantly looked to leapfrog over one another. He had thought the Court of Light was all about political intrigue, but the Court of Dark was just as bad. Every Fae was looking for a way to get ahead.

Ezekiel met Azrael's eyes with a fleeting look of shame that was gone just as quickly, as it appeared, snuffed out like a candle.

Both Fae watched as the Fire-Breathers took to the air, Construct chasing Kali. Jennara was hobbling to the platform, halfway across the ring already, satchel in hand. Ezekiel looked back at Azrael and mouthed, "I am sorry" before he took off running after her.

Jennara was twenty yards from the platform when Ezekiel caught up to her. He focused on the black satchel around her body. "Give me the egg, Jennara."

"Oh, this egg?" She pointed to the bulging bag. "Are you sure it's yours? Or does Kali have it?"

He looked up, faintly making out that Kali had a satchel; from the way it hit the dragon's body, he could see it clearly held an egg. "Troll's balls," he whispered.

"That's right—one of us has your egg and one of us has our egg, but which one?" Jennara smiled.

He went to rush her, but Jennara waved a finger. "Tut, tut. This might be your egg, and if you take it and turn it in, I win. I have a pretty good arm—I could launch this to the platform from here."

Ezekiel glanced at the platform. "If it was mine, you would have."

"Unless I am just giving Kali time to get in range to drop your egg because she has the correct one."

Ezekiel growled and rushed her anyway, grabbing the satchel, which held nothing more than a rock. "What the—" He looked at Jennara and up at the dragons.

"Your egg is back there." Jennara pointed to the water hazard. There, held between two boomerangs, was her and Kali's egg floating in the hazard.

"Why, you little troll shit!" Ezekiel glanced skyward for Construct and whistled. "Let's get the egg!" The dragon swooped down and picked up his rider.

"Now, Kali!" Jennara yelled, and Kali dropped the egg she was carrying as Jennara formed a plasma ball to catch it. Just as the egg came into range, Kali hit it with a fire breath to propel it to Zion on the platform.

Construct and Ezekiel fished their egg from the hazard and turned to see Zion catch the egg from Kali and Jennara. "No!" he screamed, but it was too late.

Zion presented the egg to Jarvok and Dragor, the egg suffused a soft blue. Dragor roared and Jarvok nodded.

"Winner by egg capture, Jennara and Kali."

The crowd went crazy; the Fire-Breathers shot fire into the air, and the night lit up, turning from navy to bright magenta and white.

Jennara dropped to her knees as Azrael rushed into the ring. Kali breathed a ring of fire around the three of them. Azrael helped Jennara up and hugged her as she cried, Kali marching around them and shooting fire into the air like fireworks.

Construct walked through the fire ring, unaffected, and bowed. "Kali, I welcome you. You fought with honor and the essence of a Fire-Breather."

Kali stood tall. The two dragons had mutual respect. Azrael knew Construct would not have taken the fight to the extreme, even if that was what Ezekiel wanted.

The ring of fire waned, and Azrael guided Jennara out. He kept most of her weight on him, feeling her back spasming.

Ezekiel was waiting for them. "Nicely done, Jennara. Let me be the first to welcome you to the Blaze Battalion."

"Thank you," Jennara said through gritted teeth. Azrael called for Kali to take Jennara. He propped her up on her dragon. "Can we get the healers to clean her up a bit?"

Healers from the sidelines rushed in, gauze and tinctures at the ready. Within seconds, they had begun examining Jennara.

"We must close out the ceremony, so let the healers tend to you. I'll be right back," Azrael assured her. He gave Ezekiel a look and gestured with his head. The two walked a few steps away. "I heard what you said toward the end, Zeke, about not wanting to lose to Yagora's trainee."

Ezekiel shrugged. "It was in the heat of the battle. We all say things we don't mean."

"Is that so?" Azrael smiled and put his index finger to his lips. "Have we lost our way? I have learned more in this tournament than I have in years. We are kin. Moving up in rank means nothing if we do not care for one another. So what if Yagora trains good soldiers? That translates into our kin being safe."

Ezekiel shook his head. "You have spent so much time in your forge, and now you want to lecture us about being kin? This *was* all about kin. What happens when Jarvok goes and plays house with the Light Fae? If it works, will we be relegated to being the hired help again? Or if we are high enough in the Guard, can we pick our assignments? Like staying here in Blood Haven?" Ezekiel pointed to the walls of the fortress. "I want a choice in where I go—it is that simple. I love my king, but I am not sure I love the idea of a queen, least of all one who used to be a Virtue. Nothing against Jennara, but this was about survival. You are lucky you have a skill no one can duplicate. I don't particularly like Pria and Yagora, but they are playing the long game, so forgive me if I am playing mine, too. Excuse me. I have to go be a good loser." He placed a hand on Azrael's back, lingering for a moment as if to convey in a touch that this was never personal.

Azrael let Ezekiel go. Ezekiel had made his point, but to Azrael, everyone seemed out for themselves and pretended it was for the good of the kin. For now, though, he was not going to let this detract from Jennara's accomplishment.

Chapter Twelve:
Blaze Battalion

The drums beat and the horns blasted as Jennara rode Kali into the ring. Jennara's armor was polished, and Kali's feathers sported Green Kyanite beads in honor of their victory. Kali would be presented with her new Green Kyanite armor tonight. Dragor and Drake waited in the center of the ring along with Jarvok, Zion, Asa, DaVita, and the High Council Guard. The rest of the dragons waited outside the ring. Los sat atop the Blaze Battalion obelisk, which was covered. He chirped and chortled to show his support.

Azrael assisted Jennara down from Kali, and she smiled, welcoming the help. "How's the back?" he whispered.

"Nothing being named to the Blaze Battalion can't fix," she said with a wink.

Zion nodded to Los, who shook his head in acknowledgment and disappeared from the obelisk, using his camouflage. The amber dragon climbed up a wall at the north end of the arena and lit a long fuse, and a moment later, booms sounded as colorful explosions of magenta, green, and white lit up the night sky in honor of Jennara and Kali's victory. The stunning firework display left the Dark Fae cheering.

Los returned to the obelisk to await his next important task, and Zion winked at him for a job well done.

Jarvok motioned toward DaVita as the bursts of light in the sky faded. The sealing of the champions' egg was the next step signifying Jennara and Kali's victory.

To DaVita's right stood a pedestal with their dragon jasper box. She held Jennara and Kali's egg aloft.

Zion spoke first. "DaVita, please place the victors' egg in their box. This egg will never be used again, for they were victorious in their endeavor."

DaVita did as directed; the long iridescent, embellished nail of her index finger glowed, and she traced the box, sealing it shut. With her nail, she inscribed Jennara's and Kali's names on the box, along with the sigil for the Blaze Battalion. "The egg is sealed, Lieutenant."

"Thank you." Zion turned his attention to the crowd. "The Crystal Keeper has sealed the egg of the victors. These are your champions!"

The arena exploded with chants of "Jennara! Kali!"

Jarvok raised his hands, silencing the crowd. "Azrael, step forward."

Azrael went to one knee.

"You nominated Jennara and Kali, a wise decision."

Yagora's eye twitched.

"Yes, my liege," Azrael said.

"It was unorthodox, though nothing about this cycle was normal," Jarvok said, his hand circling in the air as if to encompass the process. Dragor stood next to the king,

Drake behind them both. Construct brought in the Green Kyanite armor for Kali.

"True, my liege, but I never lost faith in Jennara and Kali because they have heart. Heart is at the center of everything we do, or at least it should be. For without heart, we have no passion and no love. If I ask myself if my heart is in it, the answer becomes clear. I learned that from Jennara and Kali. They act from the heart and fight with heart." He peeked up to see Jennara giving him a soft smile, her eyes glassy in the firelight.

Azrael also caught the eyeroll from Pria, but he didn't care.

"Well said, Azrael. Well said." Jarvok nodded. "Jennara and Kaliandra, step forward. You fought intelligently with integrity, perseverance, honor, and indomitable spirit. Your training has paid off, for today you will be one of only a few to be promoted into the Blaze Battalion."

Dragor roared and Los pulled the cover from the obelisk, revealing Jennara's and Kali's names as the newest members. Construct presented the Green Kyanite armor to Kali. DaVita handed something to Ezekiel, who came forward and placed two orange crystal flames on Jennara's shoulder armor. With the white striations in the crystal, they appeared like true flames dancing on her armor, and the base was made of tiger's-eye to resemble a log stoking the fire.

Ezekiel grabbed her forearm. "Chaos be with you."

Jennara exhaled. "Chaos be with you."

DaVita met Jennara with a hug, and as the Crystal Keeper pulled away, she brushed the crystal flames with her fingertips. "I knew you could do it, Jennara."

Jennara pulled out a black cord necklace holding the tiger's-eye crystal DaVita had given her. "Thank you."

Kali was trying on her new helmet; engraved on the snout were the sigils for heart and home. Jennara looked at Azrael, who winked.

Jarvok's voice boomed out, "May I present your champions of the Tournament of Fire, Ice, and Acid: Jennara and Kali!"

Jennara gazed out into the crowd. *So many Fae*. While fighting, she had not taken in the scope of the arena. Some Fae she recognized, some she did not. However, a gruff, deep voice cut through the noise, and Jennara scanned the coliseum, trying to focus on the familiar timbre. There in the front row to her left, leading the cheers, was none other than Haus.

Yes, there might be hope for Haus yet.

Chapter Thirteen:
I'm In

Jennara and Kali celebrated all night. The Marsh malt flowed, and many Polaris cherry shots were had, but Azrael observed from a distance. He was thrilled for the victors, but what he had seen throughout this process could not be unseen. Azrael was speaking the truth when he said he had learned more in this tournament than he had in a long time—and not all of it was good.

Azrael had discovered things about his friends that might save his skin one day, but that did not make it easier to swallow. He also realized that being in the forge had kept him from maturing socially. He had to make a choice.

Maybe I am not merely the Fae who implants the Elestial Blades, who inflicts pain—more than the weapons' creator. It is clear I cannot trust Yagora and Pria, and even Ezekiel has set his eyes on higher ranks; Johan is probably doing the same. Perhaps it is time to start playing the game, too. Szabo is a powerful Acid-Breather who is respected by his faction and, more importantly, Raycor. If Zion takes over Blood Haven, Szabo could move into the number-two position of the Acid

Assault. Which means we would have to compete in a tournament. Why should Pria's dragon get it?

And why shouldn't I make a play for a better position for myself and Szabo? I could be number four—or am I already? I've been in the forge, on the battlefield and have sat as a member of the High Council Guard. War and weapons are all I have ever known; it is in my blood, baked into every scar. I could retreat to the forge, create new weapons, and be left alone, but then everything would remain the same. Yagora and Pria will scheme and plot—they may even succeed. He shuddered.

As he sat in the corner, nursing the same mug of Marsh malt from the beginning of the night, Azrael knew he couldn't go backward. Jennara and Kali had taught him too much, risked too much. *I backed a tournament winner. I can still keep my sense of honor but play the game.*

He scanned the pub as Fae sang and clinked mugs. Jennara was on the bar, Haus lifting his mug in celebration of her. Haus' new eye patch was made of dragon scales to match Famina's blue coloring, Azrael noted. He heard the dragons' roars from outside as they did their own rejoicing. Then he caught the wisp of black-and-white hair in the far corner. *Yagora.*

Azrael stalked over to the other High Council Guard member. "What are you doing here?"

She moved her bangs with a quick brush of her fingers. "Enjoying a drink. I was going to congratulate you. You were correct. She won."

Azrael swatted the mug from her hand and watched it spill. "I swear, Yagora, do not even think about ruining this night for her."

I'm In

Yagora grabbed another mug from a passing server. "Relax. I have no interest in Jennara—she is of no use to us anymore. I told you it was never personal. You won." She motioned with her drink. "Go enjoy your victory."

Azrael narrowed his gaze. "What are you up to?"

Yagora chugged the rest of the Marsh malt. "In a few weeks, Jarvok signs his Unity Contract. Pria and I have until then to convince him she is best to lead Blood Haven. Your Fae defeated Ezekiel, taking him out of the running for us. That leaves Johan, and we both know he is lazy. You and Jennara did us a favor by beating Zeke in the best way possible, demonstrating his weakness—he is dumb." She hit Azrael on the arm and walked away, whistling.

"Did I get played?"

Yagora glanced over her shoulder. "I don't know. Did you?" She sent him an air kiss and waved.

Before Azrael could entertain the thought, Jennara yelled his name from across the bar: "Champs to Azrael!" The entire pub cheered, holding their mugs up to honor him. Jennara was beaming as she mouthed, "Thank you."

Azrael saluted her back. *Yeah, I'm in. These Fae are my heart, and this is my home—I can't let Yagora and Pria win. Game on.*

In the distance, Szabo roared.

Well, my Fae friends, looks like Azrael is on his way to either the darker side (no pun intended) or a new path. Jennara and Kali have succeeded in following their destiny together. I love a happy ending—and it's rare I give one, so relish this!

I hope you enjoyed *Fire, Ice, Acid, and Heart*. There are more stories to come as we explore all the hidden corners of the Veil. Each Fae has a tale to tell; you will have to wait and see whose story comes to life next, but if you have an idea, let me hear it! Many of you campaigned for the Dark Fae and the dragons, so if there is a faction or Fae you want me to write about, hit me up on Instagram: @BirthoftheFae_novel or Twitter: @BirthoftheFae. You can always let me know your thoughts on my website, BirthoftheFae.com.

I want to give a special thank you to my pups, Carlos and Penelope, for inspiring me every day. Without them, I wouldn't have the dragons or the creatures of the Veil.

Chaos be with you!

~Danielle

4 Horsemen Publications

Romance

Ann Shepphird
The War Council

Emily Bunney
All or Nothing
All the Way
All Night Long: Novella
All She Needs
Having it All
All at Once
All Together
All for Her

Lynn Chantale
The Baker's Touch
Blind Secrets
Broken Lens

Mimi Francis
Private Lives
Private Protection
Run Away Home
The Professor

Fantasy, SciFi, & Paranormal Romance

Beau Lake
The Beast Beside Me
The Beast Within Me
Taming the Beast: Novella
The Beast After Me
Charming the Beast: Novella
The Beast Like Me
An Eye for Emeralds
Swimming in Sapphires
Pining for Pearls

D. Lambert
To Walk into the Sands
Rydan
Celebrant
Northlander
Esparan
King
Traitor
His Last Name

J.M. Paquette
Klauden's Ring
Solyn's Body
The Inbetween
Hannah's Heart
Call Me Forth
Invite Me In
Keep Me Close

Lyra R. Saenz
Prelude
Falsetto in the Woods: Novella

Ragtime Swing
Sonata
Song of the Sea
The Devil's Trill
Bercuese
To Heal a Songbird
Ghost March
Nocturne

Sessrúmnir

VALERIE WILLIS
Cedric: The Demonic Knight
Romasanta: Father of Werewolves
The Oracle: Keeper of the Gaea's Gate
Artemis: Eye of Gaea
King Incubus: A New Reign

T.S. SIMONS
Antipodes
The Liminal Space
Ouroboros
Caim

V.C. WILLIS
Prince's Priest
Priest's Assassin

YOUNG ADULT FANTASY

BLAISE RAMSAY
Through The Black Mirror
The City of Nightmares
The Astral Tower
The Lost Book of the Old Blood
Shadow of the Dark Witch
Chamber of the Dead God

Broken Beginnings: Story of Thane
Shattered Start: Story of Sera
Sins of The Father: Story of Silas
Honorable Darkness: Story of Hex and Snip
A Love Lost: Story of Radnar

C.R. RICE
Denial
Anger
Bargaining
Depression
Acceptance

VALERIE WILLIS
Rebirth
Judgment
Death

4HorsemenPublications.com

Printed in the USA
CPSIA information can be obtained
at www.ICGtesting.com
LVHW091224021123
762649LV00068B/2615